The Fall of Zephyr

To my writing mentors who have taught me so much and shared your craft with me. You are an inspiration!

Cover art by Sara Freitas

VOLUME ONE:
THE HUNT

CHAPTER 1

The lavender-tinted atmosphere of the Upperworld parts as two beings march through the fog in a desperate haste. Their footfalls hit the ground and cascade over their surroundings, which is surprisingly disruptive in the already bustling walkway. Evander and Jade enter a habitation pod and begin to discuss their latest source of sheer terror – directly related to the only life they've ever known.

Since the drastic confusion involving Delphine, a young sorter who placed an orb into the wrong receptacle, and the involvement of Luna covering for her blunder, there have been concerns that the very mechanisms involving the operations of the Sorting Room are falling apart.

Luna's story, is a complicated one, as she and her intended partner, Onyx, were both meant to live human lives on Earth. Due to circumstances beyond even the Sorting Room's control, their souls were retracted back into the larger sorting system, and given the opportunity to work as immortal beings. The only problem, is that their very human attributes took over, and they still loved each other, even after their minds were wiped. Luna tried to fix Delphine's horrible mistake on Earth, but ended up with a scorned child of her own... and now that very child is chasing her, ensuring her demise at the request of Zephyr - the Most High Being of the Upperworld.

"We need a new leader, Evander. We've got to appoint someone. And soon. The future of humanity depends on it."

"What are you talking about? How? But Zephyr..."

"Is dying. His ability to map out life schemes and generate orbs is becoming less and less accurate. It's a miracle that there haven't been any more mix-ups, besides the one with Luna covering for Delphine."

Evander holds his face in his hands. "I know, but this is... crazy. There's nothing we can do. We need... a fail-safe, or something we can get to just to keep fear at a minimum."

Jade nods. "That is very true. We also need a way to explain Onyx's absence in the meantime..."

"Do you think you'll be able to cover for him? If anyone asks, maybe say that he..."

"Has a mission on Earth - yes, that could work."

"But what if Zephyr asks you? He's going to find out eventually - Onyx is a Head Guide."

Jade nods her head. "It's true, I think there's just a lot we have to account for. I also worry that these walls have ears."

Evander shakes his head. "Nope, not anymore. I neutralized my habitation pod to be a dead zone. There are no cameras or sound recordings being transmitted beyond these walls. We can use this as a safe place to talk... and to plan."

"We're going to need to rally sorters for the cause."

"And the cause being?"

"Two things: to take down Zephyr, and to elect a new leader. I have no idea who that could be, or how we'll figure it out..."

Evander looks at Jade with horror and dread in his eyes. "But... will the new leader be able to lead? Will they have the ability to generate orbs? If they don't, the human race..."

"Will go extinct."

✱✱✱

The subtle beep of the monitors slowly and steadily invades the intimate space created by Onyx's presence in Luna's hospital room. She's recovering from an unfortunate collision with an unruly truck in the middle of the night, while he is there as her protector. They are both snuggled peacefully in an otherwise cold and stiff mechanized bed, as the world keeps moving outside their window.

Ever so slightly, Luna strokes the edge of his jawline with her fingertips, a subtle touch of affection and emotion. She's comforted by his embrace, but still trying to swallow the news that she is being hunted.

"Onyx, I am really scared."

"I know."

"What are we going to do?"

Onyx pauses as a thought enters his mind, and exhales out the tension building in his chest.

"Whatever we need to do, we'll do. And we will *thrive*. Life here is… different. But not necessarily bad. I think… I hope… we'll both grow to like it here."

Luna slowly nods as he plants a chaste kiss on her forehead. As his bright blue eyes meet her deep purple ones, the pressure shifts as his lips connect with hers powerfully, nearly taking her breath away and injecting life into her all at the same time. His touch is more powerful than any drug administered by the hospital staff to keep Luna from feeling pain as her body heals. The kiss deepens as he carefully cradles her body in his own.

"Uh, excuse me. Miss… Luna?"

A petite nurse standing by the partitioned curtain of Luna's makeshift room catches the two in the midst of their moment.

"Sorry to… interrupt. I've come to do some final checks on Luna, and she'll be allowed to go home as soon as the doctor debriefs her on everything she needs to do to get better." Then her gaze shifts to Onyx as he calmly sits on the edge of Luna's bed.

"And who are you, sir?"

Onyx thinks for a moment about the proper wording for what he is to Luna. It was extremely unlikely that the most accurate explanation of their relationship would be understood in the context of earthly life. Although he personally despises the juvenile connotation of the term, being that he is over four-hundred years old, Onyx quickly blurts it out as to avoid arousing suspicion.

"Boyfriend… I'm her *boyfriend*."

The word tastes bitter on his tongue, but it is a taste he will need to acquire, as he adapts to many more things in this world that do not feel natural to him yet. Luna's eyes widen in response, as she senses some weight behind that word, even if she doesn't fully understand the implications it carries.

"Ah, I see. Very sweet. I apologize for the small space here, if I had known you were going to stay with her, I could've gotten you a cot."

Onyx shakes his head and manages a small smile. "That would not have been necessary. But thank you."

She nods politely, and then moves toward Luna to check on her vitals. With deft fingers and a polite smile, the nurse wraps a blood pressure cuff around her arm, checks the various monitors, and rapidly jots something down on a notepad.

"Okay, everything looks good here. Luna, I'll go let the doctor know you're all set."

Luna smiles, and then looks at Onyx. A smile spreads across his lips as well, and he squeezes her hand as some mild reassurance.

After a few moments of waiting, a man in a white lab coat appears in Luna's partitioned area of the hospital.

"Hello, Luna? I'm Doctor McAllister. I hear you've had a nasty accident, but it seems that you are ready to go home now. You've got a couple of broken ribs, some bruising, and a mild concussion, but otherwise, it seems that you'll be fine. Don't lift anything that weighs more than ten pounds, and don't exert yourself, at least for another couple of weeks. Luckily, ribs and concussions heal themselves, given enough time to do so. But you've got to take it easy, okay?"

Luna nods hesitantly, not fully registering the terms the doctor as using, but too embarrassed to ask.

"And I assume you'll be taking care of her?" The doctor smiles at Onyx, who is holding Luna's petite, pale hand in his own.

"Yes, of course."

The doctor nods curtly. "Okay, well you are officially discharged. I release you to the capable hands of…"

"Onyx."

"Yes, yes of course. Be well, Luna. I wish you the best."

As the doctor exits the room, another nurse comes back to remove Luna's intravenous line and various wires. The nurse briefly glances in Onyx's direction.

"You've sure got yourself a good one, Sweetie."

Luna's face frowns puzzlingly. "A good what?"

The nurse giggles. "Aren't you adorable!" She pats her on the back as she walks out.

"Onyx, can we go now?"

He smiles at Luna. "Certainly. But why don't you get dressed first? Your clothes are in the bag right there on the bedside table." Onyx points to her bright pink jumpsuit in the pale white bag with the words 'patient belongings' emblazoned on the front.

"Oh okay." She begins to disrobe, exposing her petite shoulders to the dry hospital air, but Onyx stops her.

"I'll be right here. Tell me when you're ready." And Onyx steps out to give her privacy and closes the curtain.

Luna removes her thin hospital gown and notices how frail and weak her body feels. After carrying an unwanted child, even for a short while, her midsection is bruised and beaten, and sagging in places she never anticipated. It is unclear whether the pain she feels is from the accident or her short-term pregnancy. Regardless, the pain makes it hard to pull the tight jumpsuit over her weakened frame. She manages well enough, even slipping her expelled tracking device into her pocket, just for good measure. Then she joins Onyx in the hallway, and they make their way out into the world, vulnerable as ever but determined to thrive, regardless of the circumstances at hand.

CHAPTER 2

The scorned child is resurrected in the middle of a grassy field, under a bright blue sky. His bright violet eyes hold a complex story of lies and deceit, and his body was formed accidentally in Luna's womb. The gravity is overpowering, the air cooler and thinner than he imagined. The mission he was sent with is firmly planted in his mind, while his body wavers in its new, unfamiliar environment. First he sits up, and then slowly stands. His eyes scan the perimeter of the park for Luna's characteristic long, dark hair flowing in the breeze, but she is nowhere to be seen.

This may be harder than I had imagined.

He reaches into his pocket and gingerly grasps the small dagger, and also feels the weight of the black, magnetized rock on a chain in his pocket. One was his weapon of choice for the assassination; the other, his ticket back to the Upperworld. He continues searching the park for Luna, but being unable to find her, he decides to continue walking in a different direction. He quickly realizes that he is across the street from the very convenience store that she had visited.

Maybe if I find more landmarks, that will eventually lead me to her.

Without a better plan in mind, Seth decides to do just that and keep walking. But he remains as alert as possible, lest he miss any important clues that might lead him right to her.

***

"Now Harold, I *know* it was hard to believe the first time, but I *swear* it happened again! A young boy in a pale blue jumpsuit has just emerged from the ground! No, not like in a zombie movie… I'm serious, stop laughing! Something very strange is going on here…"

***

Delphine sits comfortably on the couch watching television. The burns she received from going outside still hurt quite a bit, but the balm Elizabeth put on it certainly made it feel significantly better. She smiles at Elizabeth who is stationed in the kitchen, likely steeping some water for a cup of tea. Elizabeth smiles back, but she cannot fully hide the shock she feels from what Evander told her about Delphine's past as a demon. It shocked her to her core, and she was determined not to breathe a word of this to Delphine. At least not yet.

"Elizabeth?"

"Yeah, Delphine?"

"Is there something… I'm supposed to be doing? Or is this…" Delphine motions toward the television. "… basically it? Since you told me Evander said Miranda and Anthony are together now?"

Elizabeth smiles, even as she was still reeling from the shock of the news.

"Well, there's nothing I would suggest you do, besides just try and assimilate to Earth as quickly as you can. After you do that, there are some things we could discuss, like education or a job. But nothing yet, my dear. They indeed are together now, as Zephyr himself had intended. And that is wonderful!"

Delphine nods calmly.

"Also, um, I was wondering… why did going outside hurt me? It doesn't seem to affect you…"

Elizabeth holds her breath for a moment, searching desperately for a solution. Now is not the time to tell, if ever. But she has to tell her *something*.

"Well, everyone is different. It seems your body just reacts harshly to the sun, whereas my body does not. We'll just have to make sure you are dressed to block the sun, if you're going outside. That's all."

Delphine seems relatively satisfied with that suggestion, and gets back to watching television. Elizabeth turns back to the kitchen, where the teakettle is beginning to whistle. As she pours herself a cup of tea and offers one to Delphine, she can't help but worry that not telling her would be a terrible mistake. But somehow, just telling the poor girl she is a demon would seem both cruel and impractical as she is trying so desperately to assimilate into a culture and planet she is just not familiar with yet.

CHAPTER 3

"Well, do you have a game plan? What's the next step? How does one start a revolution?"

Jade looks down at her feet, and puts her head in her hands. "Well, I think first, we should just keep our heads down, and try not to arouse suspicion. But we'll need to gather a following. If I learned anything from my brief studies of human history, it's that the mob mentality, or 'hive mind', is often the most powerful. It is much easier to snap a single thread, than it is to break a rope made up of many threads woven together. That is the kind of power we need to cultivate in order to be successful."

Evander nods slowly, but the worry is still so very apparent in his face. "Okay, and how do you suggest we do that?"

Jade sighs. "Well, if you overhear any other sorters expressing discontent, find a way to tell them of our initiative. Then let me know when you begin to gather a following, and we'll start to conduct secret meetings. We'll need to discuss a plan of attack, as well as who should be put in Zephyr's place, since he will be dethroned."

Evander shakes his head, and forces himself to make eye contact with Jade, even though his worst fear is coming true - and he and Jade are the catalysts for it. "Okay, I'll definitely keep my eyes open for anyone who may want to join the resistance."

"Oh, and Evander? Under no circumstances, should Zephyr find out about this. That would spell disaster."

Evander shakes his head. "Well, I doubt it could possibly get any worse than it already is…"

Jade smiles sadly, and looks out the pod window. "Well, I guess now is the time to tell you… there are worse things than Zephyr falling apart."

Evander turns to look directly at Jade. "What – what would that be?"

Jade chuckles to herself, as the reality is beginning to become crazy enough to warrant laughter. "Not only is Zephyr dying, but he has the power to take us all with him."

"What? No…"

Jade nods. "Indeed. If we don't catch him before he loses complete control of his faculties… we all will descend into the Underworld with him, and be subject to even worse torture than the humans… for all eternity."

"And the human race?

"Gone."

✳✳✳

Luna firmly grasps Onyx's hand as they exit the hospital. She still has no idea about her past… because Onyx has been searching for the right time and way to tell her. It has been on his mind since the moment he woke her with a perfect kiss in the hospital room when they were first reunited.

"Onyx? What do we do now?" The sun is beating down on Luna's pale, tired face, eclipsed only by her dark-as-midnight hair. Onyx looks around at their surroundings, racking his mind for the next steps. He recognizes that they are standing in what is known as a "parking lot". *The designated place for humanoids to place their motorized vehicles while not in use*, he recites to himself. Beyond that is the busy street, and the many vehicles moving continuously through it.

"Well, this isn't... I never... planned for this. I know a good deal about Earth and its inhabitants, but I never considered that there was a possibility I'd have to - *we'd* have to, live here permanently." Onyx grabs both of Luna's hands in his own. "But I can assure you, I will do anything and everything in my power to keep you happy and safe. Let's start by getting on that bus over there."

He motions to the bus pulling up to the stop, and gently guides Luna by her outstretched hand. They both step onto the bus, but they get some odd stares. Onyx nearly forgets to deposit the correct amount of money into the depository, but the expectant glare of the bus driver swiftly reminds him.

"Mommy, why are those people dressed so funny?"

A young mother hushes the unfortunate words of her small child. "Sarah, please don't say things like that to people, that's not very nice." She offers a sheepish smile toward Luna, as the woman shrugs her shoulders. "Kids - whatcha gonna do?" Onyx smiles and nods, as he slides next to Luna on the nearest bench near the front of the bus.

"Onyx, where are we going?" Luna looks at him expectantly. Their relationship is complicated, even beyond the obvious notion of them being retracted beings who were always meant for each other on Earth, but brainwashed and reset as sorters. *I need to tell her, and soon. It is no doubt that she is beginning to wonder why she even feels about me the way she does.* Emotions are the one thing Onyx had little to no training in - because they just aren't a part of what it means to be a sorter.

"Onyx, I really don't know what's happening… do you know what we're doing?" Luna taps his shoulder, snapping him out of his long-winded thought process.

"Well, somewhat. I have some Earth currency with me, and…" He lowers his voice to avoid being in earshot of the other passengers. "There's a pool of currency reserved for Earth-bound sorters that I have access to. It's a very large sum of currency that will allow us to live comfortably for a while as we assimilate. First, I need to find a place for us to live. I'm going to have us get off the bus in a few stops. Since my embedded device has not been… expelled yet, I've been able to research available housing for us. I found a place that I think you might really like - let's go there first, and perhaps find a place we can move into. There's a lot more to do, but we can start with that."

"What else do we have to do?"

Onyx exhales in the impending exhaustion ahead of him. "Well, we need more Earthly clothes so that we fit in with the culture and society here. I'll get a job, and we'll need identification. Luckily, Evander knows someone who can take care of that for us. And there are some… personal matters to attend to. I'll explain later."

Luna nods, even though she is more confused due to what he is saying. Before she can open her mouth to speak again, the bus stops and Onyx motions for her to get up so they can both leave.

"It'll be okay, I promise. You'll see, don't worry." He places his arm around her tentative, vulnerable frame. A subtle motion meant to make Luna feel more comfortable as they embarked on their new life together. But in reality, it is just as comforting for Onyx as it is for her.

They both make their way to the main entrance of a housing complex, past a stone archway and a tranquil fountain delicately spouting crystal-clear water over an upturned stone statue of a fish, and into a pool of water at the base of its tail fin. Then they enter what appears to be a front office.

"Hello, and welcome to Aquatic Springs Condominiums. How can I help you?"

Onyx tries not to wince as the tight-collared woman in the pin-striped skirt eyes both him and Luna from behind her distinguished lenses. Their outfits definitely glean a lot of attention from on-lookers.

"If you're here for the cosplay meeting, that's in conference room 103." She dismissively jabs her thumb toward a hallway behind her.

"What? No. I'm here to buy one of your available homes."

Pinstripe-lady raises a perfectly-plucked eyebrow, as if he was asking for her to go ride a circus elephant, or something equally preposterous.

"Are you now? Well, okay then. I *suppose* I'll direct you to one of our available realtors." She picks up a phone and avoids eye contact with Luna and Onyx.

"Yes, Robert? I've got an... *interesting* young couple interested in one of our condos... okay, thanks." She ends the call and plasters a very unnatural smile over her plastic face.

"Robert will see you in a minute. Please sit." She points a manicured talon in the direction of some feeble-looking armchairs, and goes back to clicking away on her laptop.

CHAPTER 4

Seth makes his way across the busy street toward the convenience store that he recognizes from watching Luna on the Sorting Room's live feed. He is not privy to the way cars tend to drive straight down a street, so he walks straight across, causing the cars to have to stop short and angrily beep and swear at him. But of course, being the kind of terrible entity he is, Seth just keeps walking, with his determined violet gaze locked on the convenience store. By entering in there, he is hoping to get a lead on where Luna might be at this exact moment.

He pauses for a moment in front of the automatic doors, and hesitates before they open for him at exactly the moment before he walks right into them. His wordless stare carries throughout the store, as he scans the entire room for any leads on his target.

"Excuse me? Can I help you with something?"

Seth turns around to meet the gaze of the bottle-blonde store manager mindlessly tapping away on her cell phone. He fails to recognize the cultured norms of human interaction, so he holds her gaze longer than expected.

"Can I help you with something?" She flips her brittle hair off of her shoulder and impatiently taps her foot as Seth hesitates to respond. Her bedazzled name tag reads 'Tiffany'.

"I need to locate someone."

An exasperated sigh escapes from her lips without even the slightest attempt at pleasantry. "Well, have you tried the phonebook? I'm just the store manager, and I have more important things to attend to."

She quickly turns on her heel, and begins to walk away quickly in a big huff, but not before Seth notices a very small piece of paper fall from her apron pocket. He bends to pick it up after she walks away, and the bright neon pink sticky-note practically glows with excitement in the palm of his hand. In some very quick handwriting, a devilish grin oozes over Seth's face as he reads the following note:

Anthony on hold TBD
tending to Luna
Oak Memorial Hospital

He clutches the note in his grimy hand and slides it into the pocket of his pale blue jumpsuit. Without a second to lose, he runs past the fruit-flavored gum and the chocolate bars, right out the front door. The intensity and speed with which he exits certainly does turn some heads, but in the case of the aloof manager, she just shakes her head and continues being fixated on her phone screen.

Seth pounds the concrete under his pale blue boots and runs in any and every direction, before realizing that he has no idea where he is going. He quickly gets tired out and sits on a nearby bench to catch his breath.

Where do I find this 'Oak Memorial Hospital'? I bet Luna is there, and then I will end her so that my reign as Zephyr's right-hand man can begin. I just need to get there.

He continues looking around for any further directional clues, and his purple irises land on a brightly colored map. Not completely sure how to decipher it, Seth stares at it, hoping that the information would click. Minutes tick by, and the sky begins to darken, but he does not give up.

"Hey kid, are you in or out?"

Seth spins around to see a middle-aged balding man in a vest, staring at him from his driver's seat on the bus that just pulled up.

"Uh, I don't know. Is this vehicle on route to Oak Memorial Hospital?"

"That's two stops away. Get on." The driver motions for Seth to board the bus, and he happily obliges. He is about to sit down, but the driver's hand catches his shoulder and prevents him from moving forward. The slight struggle rushes adrenaline to Seth's brain and he draws his dagger for self-defense.

"Woah kid, I don't want any trouble. Put that away or I'm calling the cops!"

"Then get your hand off of my shoulder."

"I didn't mean to upset you, but you owe me a dollar for the bus fee."

Seth immediately understands that he is referring to Earth currency, so he fishes some emergency cash out of his pocket that Zephyr had provided for him. Not knowing how much is required, he hands a clump of the greenish paper to the bus driver.

"Woah kid, I said *a* dollar, not *seventy*. Come take most of this back - did anyone ever teach you to count?" The bus driver rolls his eyes and is suddenly extremely intrigued by this unique boy who has boarded the bus. Reminding himself to focus on the route, he turns back to his steering wheel and pulls onto the main street as Seth takes a seat on a blue, plastic seat by the back window.

As more people enter the bus, Seth continues to attract some odd stares, but he remains focused on his mission. The hilt of the dagger sits idly in his pocket, the metal heated by the proximity of his warm thigh. In his other pocket sits the black, magnetized rock with the subtle red glint when it hits the light. He stares out the window to keep his mind occupied while mentally preparing to destroy Luna once and for all.

"Hey kid, you wanted to get to Oak Memorial, right?"

The bus driver jabs a stubby thumb at the open bus door. Seth nods expectantly and walks rapidly down the aisle in between the seats. As he disappears out the door, the remaining passengers exchange many more curious glances, and the bus driver continues on his route.

✶✶✶

"Sylvia, you said the boy was wearing a pale blue jumpsuit, right? I think… I think he was just on my bus route… Yeah, got off at Oak Memorial, but he didn't seem injured. Yes, it's true - emerging from the ground may warrant some medical research… I still don't know anything about him, but I believe you when you said he was strange…"

✱✱✱

After speaking with Evander about the inescapable doom lined up for the Upperworld, and humanity as a whole, Jade is having a difficult time focusing on running the Sorting Room smoothly. Of course she manages to walk down each and every aisle, perusing the receptor tubes and making sure everyone knows what they are doing (what with new sorters being generated every day). With her digitized tablet in her hand, she continues taking notes on the proceedings to add to her records, but her mind continues to wander far beyond the Sorting Room. Without missing a beat, she pauses for a minute as a nearby conversation catches her attention…

"But Vidia, I understand how it works. I just don't comprehend why humans *need* us. Can't they decide for themselves who they want to love?"

The nearby guide plants her hands on her hips and shakes her head. "Humanoids are volatile, emotionally-charged beings without the foresight of the common good, which Zephyr has. If they tried to decide for themselves, chaos would ensue. Don't you see how disastrous that would be?"

The small, round face of the new recruit is filled with confusion, and a hint of… frustration. Being told to do something one doesn't believe in is a difficult pill to swallow. Jade knows this all too well, as she herself is often stuck between a rock and a hard place, as a revolution is coming up on the horizon, but her cover must remain intact… for now. Regardless, it appears that she has found the first of what she and Evander hope will be many supporters for their cause.

"Vidia, may I speak with…"

"Brielle."

"Yes, with Brielle for a moment? Privately?"

Vidia opens her mouth to protest, but nods respectfully as not to set a bad example in front of a new recruit. Jade grabs Brielle's petite hand and leads her toward a quiet area of the Sorting Room.

"You'll have to pardon my abrupt interruption, but I couldn't help but overhear that you don't fully agree with… how things are run here?"

Brielle's bottom lip begins to quiver, and her eyes water. "Oh, my apologies, I certainly didn't mean any harm, please don't punish me…"

Jade smiles at her calmly. "No, no, there are no punishments to be had. I am asking this to confirm your interest in a sort of… secret coalition that I am forming with my good friend Evander. He's one of the main record keepers in this realm, as well as a new recruit guide. Perhaps you know him?"

Brielle shakes her head.

"Well, that's okay. Regardless, I would like to invite you to join our first secret meeting at Evander's pod after the next shift cycle ends. We're going to be discussing some major changes in the processes here, and I think you'll be pleased to hear about what we've got planned."

"Oh okay, yes, I suppose I would be interested in that."

"That is what I was hoping to hear! But you must promise to keep this a secret from anyone who may not agree with you, and *especially* Zephyr."

"Oh, well, can I tell my friends? They might… we've all been talking about the same problems. I think… they'd want to come too."

Jade smiles. "Yes, of course! We need as many rallied for the cause as possible. There is great strength in numbers, and that will be our main advantage."

The small smile on Brielle's face turns into a slight frown. "Main advantage against… what?"

Jade sighs. "That will all be revealed at the meeting. Until then, keep working and doing what you are expected to do as not to arouse suspicion, and tell your friends to do the same. It just isn't worth it to attract attention from the wrong eyes. Only those interested in joining the cause should know about the meeting - that is crucial."

Brielle nods, and Jade dismisses her back to work with a wave of her hand. She cannot fight the small smile spreading on her face - the potential to win the war they are waging is bringing with it the promise of the greatest power of all: hope.

CHAPTER 5

"Hello, I'm Robert. It's a pleasure to make your acquaintance, Mr…"

"Onyx."

Robert shakes his hand as Luna stands next to him, shaking like a leaf. Meeting new people has begun to make her very uneasy, and understandably so, since her assault recently that left her pregnant and broken.

"I hear you are interested in one of our many move-in ready homes?"

"Yes, yes I am."

Robert smiles gleefully at the prospect of adding another customer to fill his monthly sales quota. Little does he know that this is step one of Luna and Onyx's new life together, and there are literally centuries of existence leading up to moments like these.

"Okay, well, if you'll follow me this way, I'll show you some of our most popular options. Let's talk budget - was there a number you had in mind?"

Onyx pauses for a moment as he tries to digest the Earth-bound terminology the agent is using.

"No specific budget. I will pay whatever it takes." At this moment, Onyx is very grateful to have access to the bank account reserved on Earth for exiled sorters. It doesn't happen often, but enough that it warranted a resource to be maintained for those who may need it to survive before obtaining a proper job to provide for the cost of living on Earth. Ironically, the 'cost of living' is heinously expensive for such a dreadful place filled with pain, suffering, and death, as Earth is.

"Well, okay then. That is fantastic to hear. I'll start by showing you this lovely model over here..."

Robert leads Onyx and Luna into a lush condo behind a very sleek, newly painted white door.

"Please do come in! This home is one of our medium-sized models with sixteen-hundred square feet of living space. You've got a fully-stocked kitchen with updated appliances, a nice sitting room for entertaining, dining room, two bedrooms, and two-and-a-half-bathrooms. Please take a moment and look around, and let me know if you have any questions."

With that, Robert settles himself at the kitchen table, and begins typing away on his laptop.

"Onyx, is this our new pod?" Luna looks around happily at the cozy home, even though it is quite unfamiliar, as of yet. But she is already beginning to find that the plush leather couches and shiny kitchen appliances are quite nice (even if she has no idea how to use the appliances).

"It can be, if you want it to be. But we should probably go see what the second floor looks like."

Luna nods, and leads him up the stairs, which are beautifully-wrapped in a soft black carpet which perfectly compliments the mint-green walls. The staircase is bent at a ninety-five degree angle, and wraps along the length of two walls. They both float up the staircase in utter bliss, with his hand in hers.

The upper hallway leads to the bedrooms and two of the bathrooms, which all appear very inviting. Feeling satisfied with this house, Onyx is ready to claim it as his own.

"Luna, do you think you could be happy here, with me?"

Luna nods.

"Okay, I'll go speak with Robert."

Onyx leaves Luna sitting comfortably on one of the beds, and he heads back downstairs to speak with the agent.

"Hello, we would like to live in this house. What do I need to do to make this happen?"

Robert grins wildly and shakes his hand.

"Well, Mr. Onyx, that is *fabulous* news! You've made a wonderful decision - this home is move-in ready, with all the furniture you see here included. Of course there are some extra fees for those features, but I suppose you don't mind that?"

Onyx nods. "Whatever it takes - I want to live in this pod."

Robert raises a confused eyebrow. "Pod? Well, okay. Whatever you hip kids are calling it these days, I suppose!" He lets out a hearty laugh, but Onyx just stares at him with his customary cerulean-gaze.

Meanwhile upstairs, Luna fingers the tracking device that was once embedded in her wrist. Since she coughed it up in the middle of the convenience store, she managed to hold onto it, but without a concrete reason.

The past few Earth-hours, she notices that it has begun to slowly, yet consistently blink bright red. She tells herself it's nothing to be concerned about, but she can't totally shake the worry from her subconscious mind.

I'm sure it's nothing. I'm safe with Onyx, I don't need to worry.

Of course, she continues to toy with the possibility of throwing it away, but there are some concerns with that, involving potential scrutiny if humanoids are to find it, as well as the potential loss of something she needs. The fact that her body had rejected it could mean it is no longer necessary, but the fact that it has always been a part of her existence as long as she can remember, makes it a hard thing to give up.

It's a piece of who I was, and who I want to be. I know I'm living on Earth now, but I was, and will always be, a sorter. That is who I am as well. Onyx has always told me to be proud of who I am, so I don't want to forget any of that.

"Well, this is fantastic, Mr. Onyx. I will file these papers and have them processed immediately. Perhaps you should go tell your wife the good news!"

Onyx reels at his title for Luna - of course, the agent has no way of understanding their complex situation, but Onyx is affected by that word and implication anyway.

"Uh, yes. Yes I will."

Onyx walks slowly and deliberately up the stairs as Robert busies himself with handling the paperwork of their transaction.

"Uh, Mr. Onyx? Just a moment please."

Onyx turns around on the stairs, and walks back over to Robert at the kitchen table.

"It's not a problem, really. But this account number you've written down... do you want me to just withdraw the first deposit out of it? You didn't specify."

Onyx tilts his head to the side, once again trying to decipher such esoteric Earth terms.

"Please take the entire amount due out of that account."

"The *entire* amount?"

"The entire amount."

"*All payments*, right now?"

"Yes."

Robert smiles politely, but appears confused.

"Well, I suppose you weren't joking about there not being a budget. Okay, then. If you'll just sign here, I will have that wired as soon as possible so you can move in."

"Move in? Where? We are here now."

"Well, I can't let you claim residency until the payment is processed. That could take 1-3 business days."

"But we need a place to stay, I just bought this pod for that specific purpose!"

Robert shakes his head.

"Condo policy, I'm sorry if that is an inconvenience. Do you have a cell phone number you can leave with me? We'll call you when it's all set."

Onyx mentally adds 'get a cellphone' onto his list of Earth things to acquire to help move the process of assimilation along faster.

"Oh, that's okay. I will come back here and check every day."

Robert slowly nods, obviously finding this to be a very *unusual* transaction, to say the least.

"All right, if that's easiest for you. We'll be in touch."

Onyx nods as Luna rejoins him from the bedroom.

"Onyx, what's going on?"

"Luna, we have to leave."

"Why? I thought this was ours now."

"It is, just not quite yet. We have to go."

Luna is visually disappointed, but allows Onyx to gently tug her out of her silent reverie and focus instead on where they would stay for the next night or two.

CHAPTER 6

Getting off the bus proves itself to be a lot easier than getting on. Seth makes his way out the door, completely oblivious to the strange stares from the other passengers. Regardless, he remains focused on his task: finding Luna and ending her life, since it was never supposed to begin in the first place. He clutches his latest clue - the sticky note from the convenience store manager. Of course she didn't give it to him purposely, but she dropped it right in front of him - and he couldn't believe his luck.

Seth ponders these thoughts and steels himself to make the kill as he walks into the main entrance of the hospital. The clean, sterile entryway seems to darken as his presence enters the space. His deep violet irises cut into the room like daggers, and he unnerves the stout, balding man who is stationed at the information desk.

"Hello, are you looking for someone?" He adjusts his strategically-placed toupée on his overly-shiny head and meets Seth's intense gaze. He falters a bit under the weight of his stare, subconsciously feeling the intensity of an assassin from another realm.

"Yes, I am looking for a girl named Luna. She has long, dark hair. She should be here." The man at the desk blinks slowly, waiting for more information. When it becomes clear that there is none to be had, he shakes his head.

"Last name? Date of admission?"

Seth intensifies his stare, and hopes that he can get what he needs through intimidation. Clearly, it is working as the front-desk worker begins to shift nervously in his seat.

"Sir, I'm going to have to ask you to either leave, or provide me with the information needed."

"I've already told you - her name is Luna, she has long, dark, hair, and she should be here."

"There's nothing I can do with that information. I need at least a last name."

"Luna is the only name she's ever had."

The man wastes no time rolling his eyes this time, and remains silent until Seth swiftly climbs onto the counter and poises the dagger intended for Luna at his throat.

"SECURITY! NOW!"

He presses a panic button, and Seth doesn't stick around long enough to find out what that means. He runs out the front door where he came and leaves without a trace. Meanwhile, the front desk hospital employee leans back in his chair, trying to steady his rapid breathing. The heavy footsteps of security quickly make their way over to the information desk, much to the curiosity and whispering of nearby patients and their families.

"There was… a young man… who held me at knifepoint asking for information about some girl."

"Description?" The hospital security officer holds a pen poised ready over a notepad.

"Well, he had dark black hair, these striking bright purple eyes like I've never seen before. Must be some of those freaky contacts or something."

The officer nods calmly. "Any particular wardrobe?"

"Um, oh yes - he was wearing this strange, almost rubbery-looking powder-blue spandex type thing. Must be something straight out of the vintage disco era."

***

Evander is happily situated in his favorite place in the Upperworld - the digital filing room. In the midst of such a chaotic upheaval on the horizon, he takes comfort in the solace of the digital files and various screens, which keep track of every being both on Earth and in the Upperworld. While performing yet another routine check, he is interrupted by a slight beeping at the secured door. He leans over to press a small green button under his desk, opening the door. In walks Griffin, one of Evander's closest friends that he has had in his almost two-hundred Earth years of existence.

"Hello, Griffin. What can I do for you?" Evander pauses his filing for a moment to give his friend his full attention.

"Oh, nothing specifically. I just came by to drop off some recent additions to the system - I have the information copied to these sorter chips - is that the format you require?"

Evander nods in confirmation. “Yes, that’s perfect. Thanks Griffin.” Assuming that is the end of the conversation, he turns back to his desk, but Griffin stays there, nervously fiddling with a stylus on the desk.

“Something else you need, Griffin?”

“No. Well, I suppose, maybe?”

Evander turns back around. “Okay, what’s going on?”

Griffon opens his mouth to say something, but then he closes it as he smiles, pulling something out of his pocket. “Well, I have this sort of personal project I’ve been working on, and I was wondering if you could help me with it?”

“Oh, sure, I suppose I could look at it in my spare time. What are you working on?”

Griffin shrugs. “Well, it’s really theoretical, but I’ve always been fascinated with the idea of time travel.”

“That is certainly a lofty endeavor.”

“Indeed, but I figure - we arrange the lives of humanoids all the time. And time keeps chugging on, regardless of what we do, for the most part. So, if we could *control* time, we could revolutionize the way the Sorting Room, and Upperworld, works as a whole. It could change *everything.*

Evander nods, and tries not to crush the young sorter’s dreams, but he also feels the need to be realistic, if nothing else. “I applaud your inventive nature and creative mind, Griffin, but I just doubt this is something that is going to lead anywhere. We can work on it for fun, sure.

But I guess I am just trying to say… don't get your hopes up. Okay?"

Griffin nods sadly, and puts the blueprints back into his pocket as Evander places his hand on his shoulder.

"Anyway, was there something else you needed to talk to me about? I'm sure you didn't walk all the way over hear to daydream about time machines with me, did you?"

Evander can sense the subtle stutter in his voice - a characteristic sign that something uncomfortable or scary is being tossed around in his head besides just excitement about time travel.

"This is going to sound weird - you'll probably think I'm losing my mind."

Evander fights the urge to disclose the crazy things he has had to deal with as of late. Swallowing that temptation, he manages to remain calm and focused.

"I'm sure you must have a good reason. What is it?"

Griffin nonchalantly walks back over to the door and closes it, until it clicks into place and the green light turns red again.

"Have you recently noticed that lately… Zephyr seems… weaker?"

The color drains slightly from Evander's face as he carefully nods, but doesn't speak too loudly for fear of the cameras stationed in the filing room for security purposes. He carefully gets up out of his chair and walks over to Griffin until he is nearly pressed up against him. As his lips get closer to his ear, he whispers only a few things to him.

"I cannot answer that here. There are cameras. Come to my pod after your shift. And bring anyone who has similar questions." Then he backs away, smiles for the cameras' sake, and nods at Griffin to drive the point home. Griffin nods curtly and makes his way back out the door he came in. Once he leaves, Evander feels a small smile of relief creeping over his face.

If others are noticing a change too, we might just have a chance to avoid perpetual damnation after all.

CHAPTER 7

Onyx gently tugs Luna away from their new home as she looks back longingly, still not fully grasping the concept of having to wait before enjoying it.

"Onyx, I really do not understand why we cannot stay." He nods understandingly, but keeps on walking with her toward the bus stop. There isn't a destination in mind at the moment, but he settles Luna's frayed nerves on the bench near their new home.

"It's just… their policy. We'll check back every day, okay? It'll be fine."

"But where do we go for now? We can't stay out in the open, can we? What if… *he* finds me?" Luna's eyes fill with tears as she buries her face in Onyx's strong embrace. He doesn't need a further explanation - he knows right away who she meant.

"Well first of all, he'll have to go through me first, meaning he's not going to get to you. Ever. And that is a promise to you, Luna. Do you trust me?"

Luna nods slowly, but her eyes drift slowly to the slight buzzing in her pocket. She knows that the buzzing is also accompanied by a blinking light, but for some reason, she has an insatiable desire to hide it from Onyx. She's worried, of course. But it's not something she wants to upset him about - there's already enough going on.

"Shush, it's okay, you're okay." He rubs her back slowly as she cries.

"I know, it's just… been a lot."

"It sure has. But I'm here now, and I'm not going anywhere."

"Onyx? my stomach hurts."

"You're probably hungry - I am too. Let's go find food. Come on."

"Where are we going?"

Onyx smiles. "There are some establishments on this street that serve food. Just follow me."

Luna returns his smile, and tries to distract herself from the concerning buzzing in her pocket.

***

"Jade! I invited all my friends to come to the meeting as well."

Jade turns around at the very bubbly voice of Brielle standing next to her.

"Oh, that's wonderful to hear!" Jade smiles but looks around to the left and to the right before continuing to speak.

"You must remember to be careful though - there are cameras and ears everywhere. Did you tell them the importance of the secrecy?"

Brielle nods. "I think so - or, at least I meant to." Jade's eyes widen.

"Make sure. This is of utmost importance."

She nods emphatically, but there is a bit of color missing from her face as she shifts her gaze slightly from Jade's penetrating stare to the area slightly behind her, maybe a hundred feet away. Jade follows her eyes and notices a very obvious group of interested sorters congregating in the middle of the Sorting Room where anyone could notice them.

"Oh no, they can't speak about that here... please excuse me, Brielle." Jade wastes no time in marching over to the group of excited dissenters. She clears her throat expectantly until they cease whispering and turn their attention to her.

"I appreciate your interest in a relatively new... endeavor that has been offered. But I need you to focus on your work." She adds in a breathy whisper: "And do not tell a soul about what has been planned." She makes eye contact with each and every one of the excited chatterers, and then leaves them to continue patrolling the Sorting Room. Taking a deep breath cannot fully calm her nerves, as what they want to accomplish is nothing short of revolutionary. With revolution, there is always an extreme amount of danger that comes with it. But of course, that means there is also the potential for great reward.

"Jade?"

She turns around once more to see the ever-present Brielle smiling ear-to-ear.

"I'm really, really looking forward to this."

Jade smiles. "I am too, Brielle. But you must not get distracted. Back to work - I'll see you in two Earth hours."

She nods, and heads back to the tagging station where an orb is awaiting the chance to live a meaningful life on Earth. As Jade watches Brielle continue working, she cannot help but think of some of the big changes coming first to the Upperworld, and subsequently humanity as a whole. They still will need to find a replacement after the deed is done - but who will that be? Jade can feel her breathing intensify again at that nerve-wracking thought. But she has faith that the sorters who are stepping up will think of something. After all, sorters are able to do what they do because of their keen sense of feeling, and knowing on a gut instinct what to do. Surely that will translate easily into a revolutionary setting. At least, she hopes that with all of her being.

CHAPTER 8

Left foot, right foot. Left foot, right foot. Pale blue boots pound the concrete, ruthlessly crushing pebbles as the afternoon sun continues its descent into evening and night. Seth continues running at full speed out of the hospital to avoid getting caught by the burly security guards that he was sure would follow him, had he not escaped as quickly as he did.

He finally gets far enough away that he feels he can safely stop to catch his breath. Crouching down next to a dumpster, Seth calms himself down enough to relax and plot his next move, since the hospital seemed to be a dead end. When nothing comes to mind, he sees his wrist glow slightly in the evening light, which reminds him that his embedded tracking device is still working, at least for now. He knows that it will be expelled from his body very soon, since Earth forms cannot support the Upperworld technology for long.

I wonder if this can lead me to Luna... He haphazardly pokes at his wrist, hoping that some random combination of algorithms would lead him to find her. To his utter surprise, it appears that his embedded device was tracking Luna this entire time, and he was just too distracted to notice it.

I can't believe I wasted all this time ignoring the fact that I had this device doing the work for me! Hopefully it stays put for at least a little longer. Although, it's interesting it can even detect hers at all - wouldn't hers have been expelled ages ago? Regardless, I can now use my device to find her.

A sly grin oozes across his pale lips, and he begins to walk in the direction that the device in his wrist instructed him to go. He presses the center of his wrist and listens for the audible directions.

LUNA LOCATED APPROXIMATELY 3520 YARDS FROM CURRENT LOCATION.

The words flash across his wrist and are also audibly said by an automated voice. A young couple wearing skinny jeans and sneakers walking by him stare curiously after hearing the automated declaration.

"It's just my communication device."

They seem to be satisfied with that explanation and walk away chattering excitedly amongst themselves, while Seth continues his mission to find Luna. He feels the comforting weight of his dagger in one pocket, and his magnetized rock in the other. One is his method of choice, while the other is his ticket home. Neither more important than the other, he feels a sense of equilibrium in his utility and importance as he continues moving down the street at a rapid pace.

✳✳✳

Evander finishes his digital filing, and slowly clicks off the main screen he was working on. After stashing his personal supplies in a locked office cabinet, he walks out the door. Pausing for the retinal scanner, he waits for the satisfied beep and then begins the short walk to his pod in preparation for the first of what he hoped would be many secret meetings.

Arriving at his pod, Evander opens the door and quickly shuts it, as he prepares to bring up the informational documentation he found about the importance of their uprising. To his dismay, he has recently been seeing documented statistics that show very plainly that the Sorting Room is failing to operate as productively as it had in eons past. Shaking his head, he manages to stay focused long enough to continue his prep work. After setting up his small 3D holograph projector, he places a pitcher of water and some simple refreshments on his little kitchen table. And then, he waits. The Earth-time clocks on his wall show all the different time zones, but he was always more interested in the North American Eastern timezone. For reasons unbeknownst to him, that was chosen as the standard for Upperworld proceedings.

He exhales slowly as he tries his best to center himself at this crossroads of the Sorting Room, and human existence as a whole. This is the beginning of the end, in many ways. But he is determined to go down fighting, and just maybe, he'll live to see a better tomorrow.

"Evander? Am I too early?"

He is snapped out of his thoughts with a voice audible from his door monitor. He looks through the digital safety lens that he installed himself, and recognizes the small smile on Brielle's petite face. He opens the door quickly and ushers her in.

"Oh no, my dear. You are right on time. Hopefully the others will be here momentarily."

Brielle nods. "Absolutely - I invited all my friends. Honestly, we've been noticing some… things lately that bothered us quite a bit."

Evander places his hand gently on her shoulder. "I am both concerned and relieved that you all see it too. Please make yourself at home - there are refreshments on the table."

"So, it's okay to talk about anything here, right?" Brielle asks her question hesitantly as she settles on Evander's pristine white couch.

"Indeed. I have personally neutralized any kind of possible signal, be it auditory or visual, from leaving the inside of this pod. Some might call it a dead zone, but to me, it's the only place I feel I am allowed to fully live."

Brielle smiles nervously. "I understand what you mean, I think. I'm still scared though."

"As you should be. Things will never be the same again, either here or on Earth."

Evander opens his mouth to speak again, but the doorbell rings and a few more dissenters join the cause. "Hello, and welcome. Please take a seat. We are just waiting on Jade to arrive, as well as any others who are interested."

As the moments drag by, more and more sorters enter his pod. When Jade finally arrives, her jaw drops from the shock of how much interest they had gleaned in such a short amount of time.

"Evander, I had no idea…"

"Me neither."

"Is this pod spacious enough?"

"It will have to be, for now."

Jade nods slowly, and then whistles loudly to get everyone's attention as she makes her way to the digital holograph projector.

"Sorters, orderlies, and general personnel of the Sorting Room. I welcome you to the first secret meeting of…" She pauses for a moment, and walks over to Evander.

"What do we call ourselves? I suppose in all the excitement, we had forgotten a name."

Evander shakes his head. "I never considered the possibility of there being this many who were interested. My pod is bursting at the seams."

"Well, I'll have to ask them."

Jade turns back to the crowd gathered in Evander's pod and nods apologetically.

"I apologize for the interruption, but I have just realized we have not decided on a name for this coalition. It's a small matter, but I encourage you each to think about that a bit. Anyway, onto why we are all here. It has become apparent as of late that the Sorting Room has not run as smoothly as it has in the past. I am sure you all have noticed that, correct?"

The small room nods in unison, with a chorus of affirmative words drifting amidst the tepid recycled air.

"Yes, Amethyst?"

Jade acknowledges the raised hand of a tall, strong, sorter, who has been in the Sorting Room nearly as long as herself.

"It has been so obvious… I have noticed a drop in both the quality and quantity of orbs generated in the past few Earth months. They have changed from being perfectly spherical and thoroughly wet, to being rather imperfectly shaped and almost dry. I have been terrified that they would get stuck in a receptor tube, which would of course spell disaster."

Jade nods her head slowly. "Indeed, this is very true. Evander, show her your graphs."

Evander nods his head as he presses some buttons on his protector remote, and brings up the data he has been secretly collecting since the very first time he noticed things were beginning to go haywire. Delphine's horrible mistake was the most notable, and the easiest to point out, but the sheer fact that she was even in the Sorting Room at all had proven itself to be indicative of an even worse truth. Delphine was never meant to be a sorter at all, and was actually a reborn demon from the Underworld. He shudders at the thought, and wonders how much he should mention in this first meeting. Evander knows all too well that the right amount of fear, when used well, can inspire real bravery and action. But too much fear can be paralyzing.

"Indeed, that is all true. And this digital infograph illustrates that concern in a statistical format." Evander continues to explain the statistics behind their concerns as the colored graphs and shapes float gracefully around the room in their holographic form.

“So, do you see it? Do you understand what this means?” Jade searches the room for confirmation of her query.

“Yes… that means…” Griffin stammers as he tries his best to choke out the words that are threatening to strangle his throat in the grasp of their horrid implications.

“… That Zephyr himself is dying, and failing. If we allow him to completely die away…” Evander looks to Jade to say the words he refuses to say out loud. Her breath catches in her throat before she is able to propel the necessary words out of her mouth.

“We will all be taken to the Underworld and suffer for all eternity. And the human race… will simply cease to exist.”

Panic erupts as the audience begins to swallow the reality of what they are saying. Their erratic murmuring and discomfort begins to grow in volume, but the soundproofing that Evander has installed in his pod appears to be working anyway. After a few moments of rapid discussion and discord, Jade manages to quiet down the crowd.

“I know, it’s a terrifying prospect. But that is why we are here. We are going to dethrone and defeat Zephyr once and for all.”

“But how will we do that?” Griffin wastes no time and asks the burning question that is likely on everyone’s mind at the moment.

Jade looks down at her feet and then blows a loose strand of her silver hair from her now-messy braided bun.

"Well, truth be told, we haven't actually... figured that out yet. But there is strength in numbers, and we are hoping that all of you, as well as whomever you feel you can trust to keep this from getting to Zephyr, will join us in this risky endeavor, to say the least."

Evander nods slowly. "I am currently in the process of looking into Zephyr's history and ascent into power, many eons ago. The past just may give us the necessary information to defeat him once and for all."

A younger sorter raises a sweaty palm into the air. "But then, who will generate orbs and run the Upperworld?" She brushes away a stray piece of light brown hair.

"We would have to appoint someone. In the United States of America, a democratic system is used to appoint a leader, and it must work well, since it is the most powerful and influential country in the world."

Jade nods. "Yes, a democracy is the way to go. Candidates can apply, and then the rest of us will vote with a ballot system, with majority ruling."

The young sorter is not impressed. "Okay, but the *orbs*. How will the person voted in be able to... generate those? Doesn't Zephyr have a special... capability for that?"

"Well..." Evander begins to search for the right words to convert his thoughts properly. "Zephyr isn't so much a generator of the orbs, as much as he is more like a *conductor* of the energy from the universe. His ethereal body is merely the vessel which the energy flows through and takes shape. The ability to be this vessel, however, is tied to a specific trait, ability, or state of being. To defeat him, we'll have to cut him off from whatever that is, and rapidly connect the replacement to theirs. This extra variable in the process can be referred to as the "critical element" of the Most High Being."

The sorter slowly nods, but Evander can clearly see that his words have fallen on nearly deaf ears. However, the problem was not that she didn't want to hear - rather, it was that her relatively new existence in the Upperworld had not given her the proper vocabulary and comprehension skills to absorb the information, as of yet, anyway.

Looking around the room, it is becoming apparent that the more experienced sorters know exactly what he was talking about - and especially, the guides. Guides like himself, Jade, and Onyx, had years of training in both Earth life, society, and history, as well as Upperworld functions and mechanics. Of course, there are different levels of learning that guides have acquired, depending on their given rank in the Upperworld - Onyx had over 300 Earth years of training before becoming a Primary Guide, while Jade had 400 Earth years of training before becoming a Head Sorter. Regardless, they all know a good amount of various different types of critical knowledge.

Finding the right one to do the most important job of all would be the hardest decision of all. For the good of mankind, and the Sorting Room, Jade hopes with all her being that they would choose correctly.

CHAPTER 9

Luna and Onyx enter a fairly large metallic building painted a couple different shades of green and purple, with some arches reaching up and over the nearly cylindrical shape. Onyx pushes the door of the diner open to reveal a room full of brightly-colored tables and food service staff busily managing the tables and various patrons. Looking around at the large room, Luna's eyes make contact with the gruff, but friendly-enough hostess. Her slightly-blonde-but-graying hair is clipped up messily, and she barks commands to the waitresses like a power-tripping dictator.

"Table for two?" She snaps at Onyx. He quickly nods, not wanting to arouse suspicion or create a problem.

"Enjoy your meal, your waitress will be right with you." She quickly shuffles away after placing the menus stiffly on the table, leaving Luna and Onyx alone together, exchanging slightly miffed looks.

"Well Luna, as you may have figured out by now, some humanoids are… more pleasant… than others." She nods emphatically, and then shifts her gaze to her menu, but it's not long before a confused expression paints itself on her face.

"Onyx? I do not know what anything on here means. What is a… pancake?"

He smiles at her and takes the menu from her.

"Don't worry about it, Luna. Although I'm a bit rusty, I remember these terms fairly well from my years of extensive Earth studies. I'll order for both of us." Luna nods, satisfied with this, and cuddles in closer to Onyx's side. Unfortunately, as she does so, the expelled communication device stashed in her pocket begins to *vibrate* in addition to blinking red intermittently. Onyx's small smile quickly fades as he feels the vibration in his side.

"Luna, what was that - "

"Hello! My name is Amanda, and I'll be taking care of you guys tonight. Can I get you some drinks to start?"

Onyx's query is interrupted by the perky arrival of the waitress, seemingly the polar opposite of the snobby and displeased hostess.

"Uh, yes. Two orange juices please."

She nods sweetly and then smiles. "Hey, I really love your costumes, by the way. Are you going to the sci-fi convention or something?"

Onyx exchanges a knowing look with Luna. "No, no we are not."

Her smile instantly fades. "Oh, I'm so sorry, I didn't mean… I'll just go get your drinks." She hurriedly walks away, likely trying to hide her embarrassment.

"Adding 'get Earth clothes' to the many things we've got to do to assimilate properly. But anyway, I felt something… move? Next to you? Is there something in your suit? What was that?"

Luna sheepishly shuffles an inch or two further from Onyx on the booth seat they are sharing, but he grabs her hand forcefully, and she recoils as the memories of her attack begin to seep into her damaged psyche. Onyx sees this change in her and frowns.

"Oh Luna, I'm sorry. I didn't mean to… scare you. But please, do you know what that was? I'm trying to look after you. That's what I came here for, you know, since - "

"Okay, here are the OJ's. Have you decided on what you want to eat yet?" The unfortunate timing of this well-meaning waitress is impeccable. Onyx shifts his eyes away from Luna's violet ones and meets the gaze of the waitress.

"Uh, yes. Two orders of the blueberry pancake plates with bacon, eggs, and home fries." The waitress nods happily and floats back over to the kitchen after collecting their menus as Onyx breathes a sigh of relief.

"Okay, Luna, you have to tell me what is happening with whatever that was. At first, I was merely curious, since it caught my attention. But the fact that you're not comfortable showing me is worrisome. I'm begging you, tell me what that was if you know."

Luna looks down at her lap as a fearful tear threatens to fall down her face. Before she can hesitate any longer, she decides to give him what he wants and show him what she has been noticing. She reaches deep into her pocket to retrieve the spindling, wiry, black mass that is still covered in her dried blood. She holds it in the palm of her hand just below the surface of the diner table, and as she opens her hand to show Onyx, the red glow of the blinking light and the vibrating begins to somehow seem even more noticeable and impossible to deny.

"Your embedded device… you kept it after it was expelled?"

Luna slowly nods. "I just… it reminded me of *home*… and I didn't want to give up my connection… to you."

Onyx slowly rubs her back. "That is understandable, and I am grateful you kept it until I found you, since I was able to somehow still track you with it in the hospital. I don't know how I would have found you without it."

Luna nods. "Yes, so that is why I kept it, and I've been meaning to get rid of it, but I couldn't quite bring myself to do it, for some reason."

"But the blinking… and the vibration… that… worries me."

"Why?"

"Well, when it is still connected to the body under the skin, it does often glow as a signal, and the vibration could be leftover frequencies that are shorting out, since it has been disconnected from you. But the problem is… it still has your identification embedded into it. Which means… as long as you keep it with you, even outside the body, you can be followed. And it glows while you're being tracked."

Luna's pale face turns a ghastly white. "You don't mean…"

Onyx slowly nods and he swiftly takes the tracker from Luna.

"I need to dispose of this before Seth finds you."

CHAPTER 10

Seth continues to look at the faint lights embedded in his wrist that are leading him to Luna to bring about her ultimate demise. The blinking gets more and more frequent as he gets closer to her, and then, without any kind of a warning, the blinking completely stops.

Is she here? Is this it?

Seth carefully surveys the area in his immediate vicinity, but there are no signs of Luna to be found. As he begins to poke at his wrist desperately to get the tracker to work again, he receives the following notification:

SYSTEM FAILURE - LOST SIGNAL

Well that is just fantastic. Now what am I going to do? What even happened to her tracker?

He sighs to himself as the panic begins to set in - he quickly realizes that he is nearly out of options. The sky overhead darkens as the evening gives way to night, and Seth realizes that he also has nowhere to stay. He shakes his head, his longish dark hair swishing around his pale face and pointed chin. The nearest place he can see is a park bench, so he slowly makes his way over there to try to get some sleep. The wooden slats are hard and even slightly damp, perhaps from a recent rainfall, but Seth manages to curl up on them anyway, as he allows his consciousness to give way to sleep. His next plan of attack would have to wait until morning. It isn't ideal, but he doesn't have any other choice.

***

Jade and Evander are quite pleased with the turnout for their first rogue meeting. After a casual preliminary headcount, Jade surmises that maybe around fifty sorters, guides, and record keepers had squeezed into Evander's modestly-sized, soundproofed pod. As they end the meeting encouraging everyone to tell their friends and get more dissenters rallied for the cause, they quickly realize that they will need another secure location to meet that would accommodate a large crowd without detection.

"Evander, do you have any suggestions as to where we can find a place to meet without arousing suspicion?"

He tosses around some options in his head as Jade helps him clean up his pod from the various trash left behind by the group.

"Well, wherever we take the group next, I would have to soundproof it first. Then perhaps split up, so that we aren't all in one localized area - that could also look suspicious."

Jade nods. "That is a very good point. What about my pod then?"

Evander looks over to her from the pile of trash he is collecting for the recycling bin.

"Sure, if you'd be comfortable doing that. That'd be very nice of you, thank you."

Jade nods. "I'd be happy to. So how about we tell people of the two locations, and I guess they can just go wherever there is room?"

"Sure, I bet that'd work. But I do have to soundproof it and take out any wiring or potential bugs. Can you let me into your pod maybe after your next shift? My schedule is relatively wide open as of late, but I just need the time set aside to secure the area."

"Absolutely. That will be fine."

Evander smiles nervously. The time and effort he has put into this revolution is easily taking its toll on him, especially with the obvious added pressure of the entire human race on the line. He shudders to think about what could happen if their plan doesn't work, but he quickly shakes it off.

Fear is paralyzing, don't let it take hold. Just do it afraid.

His personal mantra keeps him focused, and has for the few centuries that he has existed. And now is not the time to give up. Not now, not ever.

"Evander? I was talking to you."

Jade snaps him out of his thoughts.

"Oh, sorry. What were you saying?"

Jade flicks a piece of stray silver hair out of her eye.

"Well, I was thinking that we've really got to start the research process on Zephyr… to figure out his mortal weakness."

Evander runs his hand through his hair.

"Agreed. I'll spend every waking hour I can when I'm not working, tapping into various databases."

“Do you think you can? They… *he* didn’t censor anything, right?” Jade asks nervously, biting the inside of her mouth.

“Well… technically, yes, there are some firewalls. But have some faith in me - I’ve already figured out how to get past a few of them… I’m actually very close to the answers. I should know very soon - hopefully in time to discuss it at the next meeting.”

Jade pats him gingerly on the back.

“I never doubted you, Evander. Never have, never will.” She smiles at him genuinely for once, and then lets herself out of his pod. Evander turns back to his laptop, and continues hacking into the Upperworld's database system.

It’s gotta be here somewhere... I’ll keep looking, as long as it takes.

CHAPTER 11

In the deepest part of the Upperworld resides Zephyr, the Most High Being. He sits on his regal throne, with his head tilted back slightly, letting the life essences flow through him and into the orbs in the Sorting Room. His flaming hair isn't glowing as brightly as it used to, and his breathing seems labored, and less effortless. Orderlies calmly float around the Grand Hall, ready to cater to his every beck and call.

He sits on his throne while breathing, and producing new life - the same job he has had for eons. Thinking back to his deal with Seth, he considers the resurrected fetus of Luna to be his prime target. She has disrupted the Sorting Room and posed as a threat to the entire humanoid existence by trying to return to the Upperworld after being irreparably tainted on Earth. The intent of Onyx to send Delphine in her place was wrong, so *very wrong.*

Quietly, calm vapors waft through the large corridors as warm air from the outside atmosphere of the Upperworld mixes with the brisk air of the Grand Hall. Zephyr requests it to remain at a low level, as he finds warm air to be suffocating in large quantities and for an extended period of time.

The ridiculous things these sorters have attempted is so very shameful - I cannot imagine how they can live with themselves. Luckily... Luna won't have to for long.

A malicious sneer oozes across Zephyr's pale, sallow face.

Seth will be taking care of that for me, I am sure. I wonder how he is doing with it?

Out of curiosity, Zephyr contacts Seth on his tracking device. Given the amount of Earth time that Seth has been gone, it is most probable that the tracker has not been expelled from his body yet, although it likely would be very soon.

The embedded communication/tracking devices used in the Upperworld do not last long on Earth due to the distance from the main communication hub, as well as the lack of integration in the human form. These factors do not fully come into effect for about twenty-four hours of Earth-living, but they are always the reason for the expulsion of the device. The only time they last permanently is when they are embedded while on Earth, and connected to the user's circulatory system (to operate as an unlimited power source).

Given this known knowledge, Zephyr calls up Seth from his wrist. The pale lights blink clearly just under the surface of Zephyr's nearly transparent, pale skin, and then swiftly turn green as the device completes the connection to Seth.

"Uh, hello? Zephyr? What can I do for you?" Seth has a sort of exhausted lilting in his voice, likely exhaustion from trying to track down Luna all day, as well as adjusting to the greater gravity levels present on Earth.

And the beeping on his wrist had just woken him up from a nap.

"Seth, my son, you must find Luna and *end her,* sooner versus later. Do you have any leads on her nearest location?"

Seth hesitates to answer, as he knows that he currently has no distinct plan of action.

"Well… I know she is nearby. I just have to narrow down the final destination."

Zephyr exasperatedly blows air out of his nose. "Well, I need you to hurry - it is of utmost importance. There… isn't much time left before…"

"Before what?"

Zephyr stops himself from admitting what he already knows to be true. He cannot let on the truth about his condition - if he does, he will seem weak and vulnerable. Unacceptable. Rather, he covers for it to avoid suspicion.

"Before I get too tired - I need you here, as soon as you can get the deed done, so you can be my right-hand confidant, as promised. You *do* want that, correct?"

Seth inhales rapidly as he recalls the offer Zephyr had proposed as an incentive for him to assassinate Luna.

"Of course, my leader. I will find a way, I will not disappoint you."

"Good. That is very good."

✳✳✳

Onyx carefully cradles the spindling, black device in his hand and grabs a steak knife from a nearby table.

"Onyx, what are you doing with that?" Luna watches him with concern in her eyes - she is shocked and concerned about the urgency in which he grabs the knife and runs into the small room in the back marked "restroom".

Luna waits expectantly for him to return, picking at her pancakes and trying not to panic.

Meanwhile, Onyx encloses himself in the private room, and quickly uses the knife to break her device into pieces before flushing it all down the toilet. He is about to go back to the table with Luna when he comes to the sickening conclusion that he still has his *own* device still implanted in his arm. It would likely be expelled on its own within a few hours, but that is a risk he cannot afford to take.

If he was using her tracker to get to her, he could easily use mine and find us that way. I cannot risk the next few hours.

With this realization, Onyx takes a deep breath, and then carefully uses the knife to make a small slit in his own wrist right over the device. He tries to minimize the bleeding with the nearby paper towels, but it becomes very messy rather quickly.

Avoid the major artery - hit that, and it's all over. His extensive learning about human anatomy allows him to know about the important functions of the wrist arteries and their direct line to the human heart. This knowledge effectually saves him in this moment of desperate need.

Onyx also attempts to let the blood drip into the toilet and not on the floor so that no one would notice that anything happened.

Carefully, and while biting his lip through the pain, Onyx manages to ease his own device through the opening in his skin and then crush it into pieces, and flush that down the toilet as well. In the moment, the urgency of the need and the adrenaline distracted him from the pain, but now that it is over, Onyx finds himself to be suddenly all too aware of the gash on his wrist. He breathes through the pain and quickly wraps it in paper towels after washing it in the sink. He also cleans his own blood off of the knife, and then takes it back to the table where a very confused Luna sits, awaiting his explanation for what just occurred.

"Onyx, are you all right? What happened to your wrist?"

Onyx nods slowly, and nonchalantly uses the now-clean knife to cut a sizable chunk off of the cloth napkin at his table setting. He then takes the make-shift bandage and tightly wraps it around his wounded wrist, hoping to cauterize the incision before too much blood is lost or infection sets in.

"I destroyed your tracker, as well as mine. But I had to cut mine out of my wrist."

Luna frowns. "But it was going to be expelled anyway, wasn't it?"

Onyx runs his good hand through his hair. "That is correct, but it likely would have taken longer than we could risk... because *he* could easily use mine to find you also."

She senses the sadness in his eyes, and is immediately overcome with gratefulness and relief. Grabbing his forearm, she carefully examines his bloody, bandaged wrist and begins to panic.

"But you're okay, right?"

"I'll be just fine. I did this to make sure *you* are safe, Luna."

I'm still scared though. Of... Seth." Even uttering his name fills her with dread - Onyx can see that quite plainly.

"I know. As you should be scared - he is very, very dangerous. But I'll protect you, no matter what it takes. That is my promise to you, Luna." He kisses the top of her head, and then goes back to eating his now room-temperature pancakes. That's the thing about Onyx - he is tough as nails and easily adapts to almost any situation.

Luna forces a small smile, and then finishes her pancakes. She and Onyx share quiet, happy chatter, just relishing the moment when for once, they can both just exist. These moments are becoming more and more rare, so they try to soak it in and relax as much as possible before they are on the run again.

"How's everything over here? Can I get you guys anything else?" The perky waitress returns to their table.

"Everything was fine, thank you very much. I can pay you when necessary."

"Uh, okay. I'll bring the check right over, then. Be right back." She ambles off toward the front of the store to get the check, while Luna sips the last of her orange juice.

"This was really good, what do you call this?"

"Call what?"

"This." Luna holds up her nearly-empty glass of orange juice.

"Uh, that's orange juice."

"Oh. Well I like it."

CHAPTER 12

Jade walks back to her own pod to rest before her next shift. She begins to tidy up a bit, in preparation for Evander to come by and soundproof it later on. After cleaning it to her satisfaction, she flops down on her bed and feels her body begin to respond to the pressure that has been put on her. The stone-cold exterior she wears most days really is mostly just an act - but no one ever notices. The risk she is taking with Evander is monumental - literally the entire fate of humanity depends on them being successful. She doesn't usually come unglued from a task this easily, but de-throning the Most High Being of the Upperworld? That is a larger task than she is used to, and the stakes are higher than ever. For the first time in her centuries of existence, Jade actually feels fear. Even when the Sorting Room was compromised before with Delphine, she wasn't fearful as much as just alert and ready to carry out emergency procedures. This, this is *different* somehow.

She is snapped out of her silent panic with her doorbell notification slightly beeping. She gets up to answer the door to her pod, and sees the bright eyes of Griffin staring back at her.

"Oh, hi Griffin. Everything okay?"

The younger sorter nods, but he's shaking quite a bit. "I'm... okay. But just... this, this whole thing..."

Jade quickly guesses what he is referring to, and ushers him inside her pod before anyone hears anything.

"Griffin, I know how you must be feeling, but we cannot speak of this here. It hasn't been... *protected* yet."

His eyes widen and he nods, even though he really wants to talk about his fears. Instead, he opts for a hug, quickly wrapping his arms around Jade. She stiffens at his initial touch, but quickly melts into the embrace as she begins to feel her own tension and uncertainties melt away, at least for a moment. Before he pulls away, Jade uses the hug to disguise what she is about to whisper in his ear.

"I'll see you soon at the next meeting, right? Remember, it will be in this pod, as well as Evander's. Just go wherever there is room."

Griffin nods slightly and smiles politely. Jade turns back to her work, and he falters at her door for a moment, as if trying to say something else, but no words come. Griffin continues walking out the door, and Jade continues readying her apartment for the next meeting.

✶✶✶

Click, click, click. The sound of Evander's research is nearly silent, except for the intermittent moments when he stops reading to type in another line of code or to search another term in the databases. The blue light of his monitor illuminates his tired face, and the slight beads of sweat forming on his forehead - he is all too aware of how quickly they are running out of time. Earlier today, he had met with Jade and discussed how quickly Zephyr is degenerating. It is nothing short of a miracle that his accuracy hasn't faded... yet. When it does, things are going to get crazy, and fast. The difficult thing is, there really is no way to know exactly how long they have left before things spin out of control - those are the thoughts currently taking up residence in Evander's mind, which is a problem since he currently needs every source of brainpower he can get for his research. After a few more painstaking attempts, Evander breathes a sigh of relief as he breaks through the final firewall, and enters the database that would supposedly hold the answers he so desperately needs.

He clicks on a few secret files and reads them carefully, trying to remain as calm as possible even though his heart is racing. And then... and then he sees *it*. The secret critical factor of Zephyr's power is displayed right in front of him, and he nearly laughs at how simple it is. But, if he knows anything about working in the Upperworld for centuries, it is that things are rarely ever what they seem. He runs a hand through his hair and reads the file, trying to internalize a plan that could work. Then, a small, nervous smile spreads across his face - it isn't a gleeful smile, no. It is something much more dangerous - hope.

Zephyr's power... is linked to his throne? That is so... simple. I never would have guessed it. According to this database, it appears that the throne holds a massive electrical current in it that is linked to the orb production. That electrical current runs through his body and allows him to produce the orbs… just like a massive chair-shaped electrical socket.

Evander's mechanical knowledge is serving him well, as Zephyr's power appears to be even more mechanical and electrical than he ever would have guessed. It had been so easy to view Zephyr as this majestic, ethereal being, but it turns out that he is little more than an energy conductor.

If he is a conductor, that means he must have a specific chemical makeup that allows him to be unharmed by such powerful currents. So his replacement… will need to have that same ability.

With the information he now has, Evander hacks into another database, this time, the one that holds Zephyr's chemical and genetic makeup. *If there are any abnormalities in his being, I will find that here. Then, I'll have to either find someone with a similar makeup, or figure out how to alter their makeup so that they can act as the next conductor without missing a beat - it would also spell disaster, if any orbs are missed.*

The energy flow is constant, and Evander knows this all too well. Over time, he also finds that Zephyr has become dependent on contact with this current for his survival, like an external heartbeat. And that, is when Evander smiles gleefully.

Take him off the current, and it's all over.

CHAPTER 13

Zephyr breathes even more heavily as he sits on his throne. Somehow, his occupation is getting harder and harder, the cool air making his sallow, pale skin feel even more delicate and paper-thin. His flaming hair is down to a mediocre flame, and he leans back, hoping to draw some strength from the current flowing through him. Although, it seems to be *taking energy* rather than re-supplying it, as of late. He purses his slightly blue, thin lips as he taps his long, bony fingers on either armrest in unison. He raises one skeletal hand up in the air, and snaps his fingers with precision. The short, quick sound reverberates through the Grand Hall, and nearly sucks the air out if everything in its vicinity. An orderly rapidly comes, in response to his summons.

"Yes, Most High Being?"

Zephyr smiles slyly, but the light behind his eyes is long gone. "Please bring me the latest status on the Sorting Room and all routine procedures."

"Yes, of course."

The orderly runs off to get the latest information that Zephyr requested, but little does he know… that she is actually part of the resistance. When she arrives in one of the main offices, she grabs a pre-written report that Evander had given her ahead of time that is meant to give Zephyr a false-positive. If everything goes as planned, he'll think everything is fine and he'll be lulled into passivity, allowing the resistance to continue as they intend to without any setbacks. She picks up the tablet, and queues the fake report onto the screen, all the while hoping Zephyr doesn't ask any further questions about it. Giving him the fake report is risky, but Evander is a technological genius, and she has no doubt that he made it as believable as possible. She takes a deep breath, and then returns to the Grand Hall, hoping not to arouse any suspicion by taking too long to produce the report.

"Here it is, Most High Being." She tries her best not to sneer or roll her eyes while calling him that - it makes the sensitive skin inside her mouth crawl to pronounce the honorary title, but she swallows the discomfort it brings and plasters on a sickeningly-sweet smile instead.

Zephyr extends a bony hand out to take the tablet, and the orderly holds her breath as he visually looks over the bogus charts and data. He strokes his chin, and then hands the tablet back to her.

"All seems well. Thank you for fetching it. You are dismissed." With a wave of his ghastly hand, he allows her to leave, and she breathes a sigh of relief. Walking back to her desk, she types a message to Evander on her tablet, telling him of the successful ruse.

Maybe, just maybe... this is actually going to work.

***

Onyx leaves some Earth currency for the waitress according to the required amount written on the bill, and he leads Luna out of the diner. The sky above them is a shade of darkening purple, as the evening light gives way to the deep indigo of night. Overhead, the moon is already visible, and between the moonlight and the streetlights, Onyx and Luna are still able to see their surroundings fairly clearly.

"Onyx, where will we spend the night? Can we go to our new home yet?" Luna's query is met with the subtle negation from Onyx, and she nervously chews on her lower lip.

"No, we cannot, unfortunately. I'm… I'm sorry. I guess it's just how things are run here with new home purchases. We're going to have to… find somewhere else to sleep."

"Well, where exactly? We can't just sleep under the stars because *he might -"*

"Find us. I know."

Onyx runs his hand through his hair, and fiddles with his make-shift bloodied bandage from the tablecloth at the diner.

"We have to remain concealed tonight so we can sleep… without any kind of an attack."

Onyx looks around at their surroundings, desperately searching for a place to sleep as the sky is fully dark now, and it would be hard to get sleep knowing that Seth could easily find them out in the open. He turns completely around, surveying the area around the diner, the nearby shops, and the park. When his gaze lands on the park, Onyx hesitates, and walks slightly closer to examine a dark figure lying on one of the park benches. The figure appears asleep, with the rhythmic rising and falling of his chest. Onyx takes one look at his face though, and gasps. Luna calmly follows, and then recoils as Onyx quickly spins on his heel and runs back to her, yanking her along by her arm.

"We have to go. *Now.*"

"What? Why? What happened? Why are you upset?"

Onyx wordlessly pulls her along down the darkened suburban street in the night, past a few more blocks, and breathes a sigh of relief when he sees a nearby woodshed in someone's yard that has been left open.

"In here, quickly!"

Luna does as she is told, and Onyx follows her, promptly closing the door and locking the deadbolt in place.

Onyx is clearly upset, his bright blue eyes wide in a panic as he leans against the nearest wall of the woodshed. Luna walks over to him, her bright eyes also showing concern.

"Onyx… what's going on?"

He steadies his breathing long enough to answer her, but the words do not come easily.

"Seth… he was right there on the park bench. I… let my guard down, we were lucky he was sleeping."

Luna slowly shakes her head. "No, you had no way to know that, there's nothing you could have done."

Onyx hangs his head in his hands. "Well, I'm responsible for your safety, and I just wasn't thinking. I am *so sorry*, Luna. This is… harder than I ever imagined. And now you're sleeping in a shed, and I just… assimilating isn't going as smoothly as I had hoped."

Luna wraps her delicate arms around Onyx's heaving torso, as he is still stuck in a wild panic.

"If he finds you, you'll be destroyed, Luna. I cannot, I *will not*, let that happen. But I'm quickly realizing, that he will find us no matter what I do. Because he is close, and will find us one way or another."

Luna nods, her lower lip trembling as her eyes begin to water. "I really do not want to be found."

Onyx nods. "As long as you don't want to be found, you'll stay alive. That's the difference - those who are captured give up hope. Hope is your best weapon right now, Luna."

She forces herself to smile, and buries herself into Onyx's shoulder. He pulls her small, frail body closer to his, until they are tightly pressed together, leaning against the far wall of the shed. Their heartbeats synchronize as one, and Onyx fights tears in his own eyes. They hold each other close, and then slowly slide down the wall so they are both sitting on the hard, wooden floor of the shed.

"Onyx, if he was sleeping, why didn't you just… take care of him then?"

He shudders at the thought of what Luna is implying. "Well, that is a very good question. I…" His words falter as he shifts his weight from kneeling on his knees to sitting flat on the floor, legs outstretched in front of him. A quick exhale precedes the words that he'd rather not say.

"I've never... been trained for killing. I don't completely know how, and even if I did, I don't think I really could. It's not... part of my job description."

"Well, neither is... any of this." Luna waves her hand around her face, implying both her own assimilation, and hiding in a wood shed overnight. Onyx frowns, and chews on the skin inside his mouth a bit.

"That is true, and I'm starting to realize that... I might have to, in order to protect you. We can't... run forever."

Luna slowly nods. "I want to just... live. That's not... too much to ask, right? I just... want to live without fear."

Onyx pulls her closer to him, and they both sit in silence for a moment before he answers.

"I don't know, Luna. I really wish I knew."

CHAPTER 14

Jade settles in for another shift in the Sorting Room - armed with her clipboard, and her wits about her, she is ready to manage the organization of human souls into their intended bodies. Upon a quick glance around her vicinity, everything seems fine, so she opts to go find Evander to check on the research progress. Leaving the Sorting Room for a quick minute, she makes her way to Evander's main office. She hits the button next to the door, which notifies him, and he unlocks the door for her.

"Oh Jade, I wasn't expecting you. Aren't you in the middle of a shift?"

Jade smiles at him slightly, and nods her head. "Yes, technically I am, but everything looked fine so I wanted to check on these... more *important* matters."

Evander moves over to his tablet where he's been keeping all his notes. "I found... some answers. It's... still a massive risk, but I think I know what we have to do now."

Jade joins him at the far end of his desk and leans over his shoulder.

"Well, here's what I've found, anyway."

She reads the articles Evander had pilfered from the secret digital files previously protected behind firewalls - but Evander, being the tech genius that he is, broke right through them. Her eyes widen as the realization hits, and she excitedly squeezes his shoulder.

"So… that's it then? Just have to get him off the chair, and find a replacement?"

Evander nods. "But bear in mind, that will all be easier said than done. Zephyr is still a powerful being, and he has safeguards set up to prevent a revolution from occurring."

Jade sighs. "I know, but… this is hope, right?" She switches gears for a moment. "Wait, what do you mean by… 'safeguards'?"

"Well, that's a broad term, and in theory, it could mean virtually anything. But one example of this would be that if he is to fail completely, we would all be…"

"Sucked down into the Underworld with him."

Evander nods. "Yes, that's one. It is *supposed* to prevent an uprising, given the understanding that if he goes down, we all go down with him. But upon further analysis, I've found that it actually *supports* the argument of an uprising, as we all know too well now."

Jade looks down at her feet and then back to the screen of Evander's tablet. "Well, looks like we're on the right track then."

"I'd say so."

"Did you get a chance to soundproof my pod yet, by any chance?"

Evander holds his face in his hands. "I knew I was forgetting something! I know the meeting is soon, but I had been too wrapped up in my research, that I guess I forgot. I'll go do it now. Sorry about that!"

Evander gets up to go to Jade's pod, and grabs his tool belt and various bug-detecting gadgets. He is about to close down his computer and turn off the light in his office, when Jade gently grabs his arm.

"Evander?"

He stops to meet her gaze.

"I just wanted to say, with everything that is going on, that I think you… are amazing. And I couldn't… I couldn't do this without you."

Jade carefully wraps her arms around Evander's torso, and he freezes up, not used to this sort of reaction from her (or anyone, for that matter). After a moment of her awkward embrace, he gently pulls away and nods at her. They both exit his office, and part ways until the next meeting of the "Disturbers", as the revolutionaries have begun to call themselves. Jade heads back to the Sorting Room, and Evander goes straight to her pod to complete the soundproofing necessary for their meeting.

✳✳✳

The dark-haired child awakens from his slumber on the park bench. His back is noticeably stiff, and there's a crick in his neck from lying down on the hard, wooden surface for so long. Seth manages to sit up, and stretch, wincing slightly at the unfamiliar popping in his joints. After a few deep breaths, he remembers the orders from Zephyr - that he needs to find Luna as soon as possible.

Tapping on his embedded communicator, he tries to track Luna, but to no avail.

That is so strange, I wonder why it isn't working? Seth shakes his head in frustration.

He stands up, trying to plot his next mode of attack, but a sharp, quick shooting pain in his wrist causes him to quickly sit down again. As quickly as it begins, it ends, but almost immediately turns into a palpable, Earth-shattering form of nausea. His insides begin to churn, and he soon feels something slowly and agonizingly making its way back up his throat. Pushing, gagging, gasping for air, he finally manages to spit out a spindly, black mass of wires as the nausea subsides. On an impulse, he immediately looks at his inner left wrist… and his device is indeed gone.

Well, not totally gone - it's technically right here, but now it is utterly useless. The bloody, black mass of wires sits in the palm of his hand now, suddenly feeling strangely foreign. He throws it angrily into the nearby reservoir, and then turns, walking toward the nearest restaurant. The loss of the device is significant, but so is the discomforted feeling of hunger in his stomach. In response to the giant, orange sign advertising "food", he enters the retro diner, hoping to satiate his hunger as soon as possible so he can find Luna and carry out what Zephyr had intended.

✳✳✳

"Harold, look! He's here!"

"Who's here?"

"That peculiar blue-jumpsuit fellow. He's sitting right over there."

Harold nearly chokes on the bite of pancakes he stuffed in his mouth. "What? What is he doing here? What does he want?"

"How would I know?"

"I'm going to go talk to him."

"Harold, be careful! What are you going to say?"

"I'll ask him what business he has here! I get a bad feeling about him being around town. Something about him is very off-putting."

"I agree but don't upset him! The last thing we need is for him to attack you or something…"

"He's not going to attack anyone, Sylvia."

"You don't know that!"

"I'm gonna go talk to him. Sit tight."

CHAPTER 15

The nearly dead silence of the Grand Hall is deafening. Zephyr sits nonchalantly on his throne, but his entire body is heaving as the current of life forces flow through him. The very energy that used to fuel him is now sucking the life from him. He knows he doesn't have much time left, but somehow, he continues functioning.

The orderlies in the Grand Hall have stopped coming to his every beck and call, and he is beginning to see that his presence was becoming less and less important. The thought makes the flaming tongues of hair stand up taller on his ghastly forehead, a white slope into the abysmal recesses of his deep, dark eyes.

He straightens his back against the throne, and his long, wiry fingers tightly grip the edges of the armrests. What once felt regal and all-powerful is finally beginning to feel ordinary and weak. The changes happening are all too shocking and much too fast.

This cannot be the end. Not yet. Seth has to help me. Once he gets rid of Luna, he'll be able to join me, and I can feed off of his life-force for all eternity. But it has to happen soon.

Zephyr groans under both the metaphorical weight of his own lofty expectations, as well as the pressure of the entire Upperworld and by extension, the future of humanity.

Every minute Luna lives, I get even closer to ultimate demise. But they will soon learn what happens when they defy me - all of the sorters will see that we are tied together, for better or worse.

✱✱✱

Luna awakens in the woodshed, in Onyx's strong arms. He is still asleep, his head leaning back against the wall of the structure. His slightly pink lips twitch slightly in the later stages of sleep, and Luna feels the corners of her own mouth turn up in a smile as she gazes upon the face of her one-and-only. Their relationship is unusual, sure. But their connection is so strong, that even the mind-washing strategies of the Upperworld could not erase what was already embedded in the essence of their souls.

She brushes a stray piece of his pale blonde hair off of his forehead, and carefully places a small, chaste kiss on his temporarily-unconscious lips. He quickly awakens from his slumber, and responds to her kiss wholeheartedly.

"That's a very nice way to wake up."

Luna smiles at him. "And you're a very nice person to wake up with."

Onyx wraps his strong arm around her tired shoulders and holds her close.

"Onyx, what's next? What do we do now?"

He strokes the long tendrils of her dark-as-midnight hair as it cascades down her back.

"Well, I can check on our new home and see if it is ready for us. And then, we'll need to do some rapid assimilation to the society on Earth."

"Like what?"

Onyx thinks for a moment. "Well, for starters, these clothes are not suitable to blend into society with. We'll need to go to a vendor and buy clothing more becoming of people on this planet."

Luna frowns. "Well, I really like my clothes. They are comfortable and all I've ever really known."

"I understand that, but we've got to start blending in more. We're all too easy to spot, both by Seth and any curious humanoids."

"Are the humanoids going to hurt us?"

"Well, no, I doubt it, but -"

The door of the woodshed abruptly opens to reveal a very angry looking man with a long, ruddy beard rolling a wheelbarrow.

"Hey, who are you? Get out of my shed! What the hell is wrong with you? Don't make me call the cops!"

Onyx immediately stands up and drags Luna with him.

"My apologies, sir, we just needed -"

"I don't give a flying fig what you needed! Just *get out.*" His mandate is accompanied by a sharply-pointed finger emphasizing their need to get away. Onyx quickly nods and motions for Luna to follow him.

"That's right, you *better run*!"

The shed owner does not appear to be chasing them, but he continued to waggle his finger and yell at Onyx and Luna even though they are clearly on their way to get off his property.

"Onyx, why was that humanoid so upset?"

"Well, it seems I made an error and housed us in a structure that belongs to him. Granted, I didn't have much of a choice at the time, but given the laws that govern this world, I should have been more thoughtful."

"So some humans have ownership of an area of the Earth?"

"Precisely."

"But the Upperworld isn't like that."

"That is true."

"Why is it different?"

Onyx looks off into the distance, where the mid-morning sun is well into its steady ascent to its projected zenith.

"Well, I do not know. There are many things that I don't know about Earth, even though I have studied humanoid life for centuries. History and culture changes all the time, and it is all too easy to miss out on subtle nuances within Earth's societal norms."

Luna nods slowly, even though she likely cannot absorb all the information he is conveying to her. For a being who is still relatively young, despite her recently discovered reproductive abilities, there is still much to be learned.

"So, what now?"

"Now, we assimilate."

CHAPTER 16

"Wait, so how is this going to work again?" A young sorter raises a hand, interrupting Jade from explaining their latest findings. Jade smiles politely but very obviously holds back a frustrated grimace.

"Well, Zephyr's source of power is the current that flows through his throne, and if we get him away from that, we can more easily overtake him."

The sorter nods slowly, her auburn curls bouncing nervously. "Is this… really going to work? Will we be… okay?"

"That's up to you."

"What do you mean it's up to me?" The young sorter's face turns white with the fear of what Jade's implication could mean.

"It's up to you, and you, and you. All of us must work together to accomplish our goal."

Nervous murmurs fill the small common area of Jade's pod.

"Now don't let this paralyze you, whatever you do. This mission is not one that can be accomplished under the pretense of fear. Fear is your worst adversary - defy fear, and you can defeat Zephyr."

The group begins to react to her empowering words with exclamations of concord. The murmurs turn into excited chatting, and only a few sorters are left still concerned, based on the worried looks on their faces. Jade is unflappable, however. She never lets the concerns of others distract her from what needs to be done, and right now, she must stay focused on the task at hand and avoid getting too personally involved with the worried sorters at all costs.

"Where are Evander and the others?"

"They are meeting at his pod - there are too many of us now to fit in one place. But that is a very good sign. We must grow in numbers to increase our chances of success. I implore you, speak with anyone you know who is interested in the cause, but use caution - if Zephyr, or any of his servants hear of our plans, he has the power to immediately enact mass destruction."

The crowd goes silent, trying to swallow the reality of what Jade has warned them about.

"So you really mean, that at any moment, he could just drag all of us down to..." The sorter bites his lip, too afraid to say out loud what he is assuming to be true.

"The Underworld? Yes, indeed. Which is why we have put safety measures into place, such as the high-quality soundproofing and neutralizing that Evander has provided, both here and in his own pod. *And* you must be careful what you tell the others. However, they need enough information to know where to meet us, so use your discretion to figure out how much to tell them."

***

"And then what? What happens after Zephyr is dethroned? Who is going to run the Upperworld?" Evander pauses for a moment before answering the question of the seasoned sorter who stands slightly taller than most of the others.

"That, will be up to us to decide. After researching methods of governing this decision, Jade and I have found that the democratic method of voting - commonly used in the United States to choose a presidential candidate - should work quite well. Following their example is a wise choice, since it is common knowledge that the United States of America is the strongest, and most influential country on Earth."

"Okay, so who are the candidates?"

"We still need to decide that. So, I've put together some forms here. Please write down the names of anyone you think would be able to handle the most important position in existence. Do *not* take this lightly - your future, and the future of humanity, depends on your careful decision-making."

"But how do *we* decide?" Another record-keeper raises her hand. "I've studied records and statistics of many sorters, but no one stands out to me as being able to handle it. How do we know?"

"Well, we don't, and won't know for sure, until we try. It's going to take a leap of faith. *But*, some things that you may want to consider are the following:" Evander points to the next page of his holograph presentation, and waits patiently for the entire crowd to settle down before continuing.

"Consider the knowledge a given candidate has about Earth, humanoid life functions and processes, as well as ethics, obligations, and adaptability. Does this person know both how the Upperworld functions, in conjunction with how Earth functions? Who do you know that has extensive knowledge in both areas? If you can think of someone that fits that description, then you've got a strong potential candidate to be the Most High Being."

"There's not many of us that can boast of knowing enough about both the Upperworld *and* Earth." Another younger sorter joins the conversation.

"Yeah, the only one I can think of would be Onyx…" A friend of that sorter nods next to him, and pats him on the back for added emphasis. Then the murmurs begin to fill the room again. Evander clears his throat to get their attention again.

"Well, as you may know, Onyx is… unavailable at this time."

"For how long?"

"Well, indefinitely."

"Where is he? What happened?"

The questions the sorters ask are quite private and require what Evander commonly refers to as a "high level of clearance", but given the magnitude of the situation in conjunction with their dire need, he quickly decides to just briefly explain what was going on.

"He had been sent to Earth to protect Luna. I don't know if you all had heard about the various problems surrounding that horrendous mix-up in the Sorting Room, but it is related to that."

Brielle pipes up, her bright eyes shining in the low light of Evander's pod. "Well, bring him back then! Since he's been to Earth, and survived there for a while, I bet he's the most qualified for the job."

Upon hearing her suggestion, the rest of the crowd begins to mumble their accord, with their voices steadily growing stronger and louder as the idea takes shape in their minds and carves out a home in their hearts.

Evander opens his mouth to speak, but quickly realizes the reality that Brielle has so effortlessly brought to his attention: Onyx really *is* the most qualified member, and by a long shot. No one else can boast of extensive Earth training, Upperworld knowledge, *and actual experience* surviving on Earth. Dumbfounded, he shakes his head in disbelief - how did he not see this before?

"Brielle, you are absolutely right. I will speak to Jade about this immediately and see what we can do. So, is there any need to vote? Or perhaps I'll just propose - all those in agreement that Onyx should be the Most High Being of the Upperworld, and oversee all functions of orb production and the resulting humanoid lives, say 'I'."

He barely finishes that sentence before the entire room explodes in a chorus of "I's", and he realizes that the right choice was right in front of him all along - he had just been too wrapped up in his research to see it.

CHAPTER 17

Seth is seated at the retro diner, looking through the menu, even though he has no idea what any of it actually is. He continues mindlessly staring at it, hoping to decode something before the waitress returns to his table.

"Hey kid, I've been seeing you around, and I gotta know… what's your business here?"

Seth looks up from his menu to see an older balding man wearing faded jeans and a beige cardigan sweater. His gray eyes peer condescendingly down at Seth from behind his black-rimmed reading glasses perched low on the bridge of his nose.

Seth meets his gaze and stares at him with equal intensity. "I am here to ingest some food."

The older gentleman waggles a finger in his direction. "Nope, I really don't think that's it. I saw you on the bus threatening the driver…"

Seth looks at him, shooting daggers out of his narrowed eyes. Then, only a mere moment passes in complete silence before Seth gets up from his chair and places his blade at the man's throat, all in one fluid motion.

His wife shrieks from a nearby table and the other patrons stop their conversations to see what is unfolding in front of them.

"Hey, hey kid, I didn't mean any harm, I just, I just…" Seth tightens his grasp, and applies some calculated pressure to the dagger, calling forth a bead of blood to appear.

"Leave me alone, or I will shove this blade through your critical artery and never look back", Seth explains through his gritted teeth.

The man, terrified, slowly nods. Then Seth releases him from his grasp, and runs out of the diner before anyone can detain him. He is not privy to Earth law enforcement, but he is smart enough to know that the uproar he unwittingly caused would easily be enough to get him into trouble if he sticks around.

Meanwhile, the older man catches his breath and his wife clutches him while crying hysterically.

"He… he could have *killed* you, Harold. Why would you upset him like that?"

"I didn't mean to… I really just wanted to know what he was up to, I had no idea he would pull something like that!"

"But you saw him threaten the bus driver?"

"Well, that's true, but I didn't think- "

"See, that's just your problem, Harold - *you never think!* And one of these days, you are going to get yourself killed!"

"Sylvia, if this is about the toaster I left plugged in then - "

"No, well, yes, but no! I just, can't stand to see you act like such an imbecile! I don't know what I would do without you! So smarten up!"

Harold sighs as he finally begins to catch his breath. His pulse rate is still heightened, but he is confident it will settle down within a few minutes, at least now that the crazy kid was gone.

"Um, excuse me, Sir?"

Harold turns around to see one of the waitresses standing with a fully-decorated police officer, who is armed with a fully loaded utility belt and a notepad.

"I'm here with Officer Carnes, and he'd like to ask you a few questions about what happened. And… your breakfast is on the house, as small compensation for the…. uh, traumatic event that just occurred."

"Oh, uh, that is very kind of you. Sure, I'll answer anything you want to know about that blue-jumpsuit character. My wife and I have both been seeing him, and others similar to him, around town, and it is quite unsettling, to say the least."

"Oh, so there has been… more than one?" The officer's interest is clearly piqued, even beyond his profession.

"Well, not violent like that one, per se, but there's a female character in a pink jumpsuit, and another male one in a blue one. Maybe some sort of cult, I don't know."

***

Eyes closed, Zephyr leans back in his throne. He is no longer able to move without expelling an inordinate amount of energy, so he sits there. The current continues to flow through him, and the orbs continue to be produced, but it is getting harder. Zephyr tries to remain calm, but he knows his time is coming - and soon.

In a moment of sheer curiosity, Zephyr manages to pry his eyes open for a moment, to see what is going on in the Grand Hall. Per usual, nothing at all exciting is happening - it is just the routine patrols of his workers and keepers. After a quick perusal of the area, he succumbs again to the heaviness of the eyelids covering his dark, abysmal eye sockets. The rest of his body lies vulnerably on the throne, seemingly waiting for him to be overtaken by his weaknesses.

But he is not going down without a fight - not here, not now.

CHAPTER 18

"Onyx, where are we going now?" Luna looks up at him with her big, bright purple irises.

"To a vendor that sells a wide variety of humanoid garments… it is called 'the mall'. We are going to procure as many as we need, so that we can better blend in to the society here."

"Okay, but I might feel strange doing that."

Onyx raises an eyebrow in confusion as they walk, hand-in-hand, down the street to the mall. "What makes you say that?"

"Well, we don't belong here…"

Onyx stops dead in his tracks and looks at Luna. His cerulean eyes meet hers, and he places a hand on each of her shoulders.

"I understand this is difficult for you, but it is necessary for us now. We *do belong* here now, Luna. We just need time to get used to it. More specifically, you must grant yourself ample time to get used to it. Can you do that for me?"

Luna nods her head, and a small smile appears on her lips. "I can try."

"That is all I ask!" Onyx smiles back at her and grabs her hand, continuing to lead her toward the mall.

Upon entering the mall, the duo is met with a plethora of stores and styles to choose from, but Onyx uses his mental database of Earth knowledge to figure out the latest styles.

“Luna, we must find some new clothes for you, let’s try this store here. According to my research, this vendor is very popular among the female humanoids within your age bracket.”

“Onyx, how old am I?”

He pauses for a moment, trying to process what she asked in terms that she could understand.

“Well, you do not have a fully established age the way humanoids do, but for our purposes, based on your body composition and appearance, just say you are twenty years old, should anyone ask you. It’s far too complicated to entertain any kind of story different than that.”

Luna nods her head.

“Oh and Luna? I suppose now is the time to tell you that… you will *age* here. That means your body will deteriorate a bit as the years go by. Granted, that is a while away, but I don’t want you to be shocked.”

Her face turns pale. “Will it hurt? Will I recognize myself? Will *you recognize me*?

Onyx pulls her close to him and strokes her back. “Of course I will, Luna. It is a gradual process, so I’ll always know who you are. And… I will age too. Everyone does. But it’s okay - a lot of humanoids have been able to age gracefully - we’ll be able to do the same, you’ll see.”

The younger girl’s lower lip begins to tremble, but Onyx pulls her into a tight embrace.

“It really is okay, you’ll see. Please do not worry! I’ll always be, right here. Just trust me.” Onyx smiles at her, his bright white teeth glistening in the bright fluorescent lights of the clothing store.

"Okay, now let's get you some clothes." The two of them begin trying many different things off of the shelves, until deciding on a vast array of jeans, sweaters, tee shirts, and shoes for Luna.

"Onyx, does this look okay?"

Luna emerges from the dressing room in a very pretty yellow sundress, paired with some black leather gladiator sandals. The dress fits her perfectly, and Onyx's jaw drops.

"Luna, you look absolutely *radiant.* Add that one to the pile, we must get that one for sure."

She smiles gleefully and closes the door to the dressing room to try on the next outfit Onyx had pulled for her. Luna has no idea how to style herself in a way that would allow her to properly assimilate, so she let Onyx pick out her clothes based on his knowledge of Earth popular culture.

"Oh my gosh you're like, so sweet to take your girlfriend shopping!"

Onyx turns around to see a younger girl, perhaps around fourteen years old, smiling at him through some neon-pink braces and blue-rimmed glasses. Her wild, curly red hair is pulled into a messy ponytail and peeks out from behind her head.

"Uh, sure. She just... needed some new things." Onyx rubs the back of his neck while staring at the floor. Getting noticed by humanoids is still a very unsettling experience, even though he knows that he will have to get used to it eventually.

The younger girl smiles and waves at him, and then she catches up with her mother perusing the sales rack nearby. Onyx allows a small smile to escape from his lips, while thinking about how lucky he is to have Luna all to himself, forever and always.

"Onyx? How's this?"

He snaps out of his silent thoughts to see Luna in a pair of gray fitted jeans and a deep purple sweater which perfectly compliments her eyes while her long, dark-as-raven's-feather hair cascades in loose waves down her back.

"It's perfect - add it to the pile!" It is undoubtedly a bit strange seeing Luna look more and more like her humanoid counterparts, but Onyx is also quite pleased that she seems to fit in perfectly - that is a key component of successful assimilation, as he knows all too well.

After some time looking for her new outfits, Onyx does the same, and they reconvene to pay for everything and leave the store. Onyx walks out of the store wearing black jeans and a red-and-black flannel shirt layered over a tee shirt of a band he doesn't know, while Luna decided on a pair of pink jeans and a ruffled blue blouse. They both have swapped their clunky boots for more comfortable, light-weight sneakers and socks. Armed with bags of new clothes, and other needed personal items that Onyx had said they might need, they enjoy the rest of the mall trip immensely - at least until Onyx remembers something slightly uncomfortable to attend to.

"Luna, there's something *else* we should get for you." She turns to meet his eyes and smiles, but the uncomfortable frown on his face suggests something slightly awkward is brewing under the surface.

"What's that?"

"Just, uh, follow me."

Onyx gingerly grabs her hand and leads her toward a store that he only knows about from his humanoid research - the specialty lingerie store.

Luna looks around confused, so Onyx awkwardly explains the best he can after taking a quick breath.

"Girls here… they wear things *under* their clothes. To fit in, you'll have to do the same." He avoids her gaze and calmly leads her into the store. Luna looks around at all the mannequins with wide eyes, not quite understanding the contraptions on their bodies, but curious about what it means for her.

"Hi, may I help you?" An overly-perky employee with medium-brown hair and a sparkly pink name tag smiles at Luna, and looks at Onyx questioningly.

"My… girlfriend needs a… fitting." Onyx searches his mind for the right terms, and sighs in relief when the employee nods.

"Certainly! Right this way." Luna looks at Onyx with tangible fear in her eyes.

"I'll be right here, Luna." Onyx tries not to stare at the outlandish undergarments on display, and goes over to the nearby couch to stay as far away from the center of the feminine specialty store as possible.

"Oh, that's your name? How pretty!" The shopkeeper's voice trails off as she leads Luna to a nearby dressing room.

CHAPTER 19

"So, how was your meeting?" Jade asks Evander while they both walk to their respective workplaces from their nearby housing. They have to watch what they say, of course, since they are out in the open without any soundproofing.

"Oh, it was good, I think."

"Good!"

"Indeed."

To avoid arousing suspicion, Evander stages a fake trip, and leans discretely toward Jade., to whisper in her ear: "Let's meet later, just you and I, at my pod, please. Something happened that we should discuss."

"Oh Evander, get off of me! You are so clumsy." She frowns and shoves him away, pretending to be annoyed at him for "falling" on her, and then nods nearly imperceptibly.

"See you then", she whispers back.

Evander continues walking toward his office, as Jade heads in the opposite direction toward the Sorting Room. He inhales, and then exhales, relishing the feeling of the calm, tepid air of the Upperworld filling his lungs. It is so easy to wonder, how much longer would they have before everything began crumbling down? Based on his own meticulous calculations, and data entries - probably not very long. Zephyr is getting weaker every moment, and it is only a matter of time before everything unravels.

***

The scorned child catches his breath a few blocks away from the diner. He had been running, as the people there had questioned him, and they didn't seem to take too kindly to him defending himself.

Earth is so strange. Why do people challenge me like that? They will quickly realize that I am not one to upset.

He shakes his head, and then realizes that he is still very hungry - and thirsty, for that matter, since he never did get a chance to order food before he was questioned. Seth doesn't even know why they were so concerned about him being there, but regardless, his presence seemed to be quite a disturbance.

The mall... maybe I can find food there? Without any better options presenting themselves, Seth enters the mall, slowly and deliberately making his way across the parking lot. A few cars swerve to avoid him, because he keeps his head straight ahead, moving toward the building like a shark to its prey. His very essence is unsettling - his eyes glaze over with their piercing violet gaze. Nearby, families pass him as he makes his way to the mall entrance, and the children stop, stare, and point as their parents embarrassingly avert their stares and try to redirect their children. But Seth does not falter, or even hesitate. He makes his way over to the mall entrance, and continues in, looking for the first sign of food.

While walking through the mall, Seth walks past many stores, some stranger than others. In fact, he finds himself standing in front of a *very* strange store, one sporting lots of pink and strange models wearing very little clothing - rather, it appears to be that they are wearing some strange contraptions of some sort. He is not familiar with such items, so he stops to look, and that is when he sees something *extra intriguing.*

In that strange store of pink and uncomfortable-looking oddities, he spies a man with spiky bleached-blonde hair waiting on a nearby bench at the side of the store. *Is that... Onyx? If it is, then Luna must be close! Although, he isn't wearing his typical pale blue clothing... maybe he obtained new Earth clothes? That is possible. I don't want him to see me yet though...*

Seth continues walking toward the store, looking for Luna. He enters the store without being detected by Onyx, but is so distracted that he nearly knocks over one of the scantily-clad mannequins.

"Hello, sir. May I help you find something?" A perky store employee locks eyes with Seth, who immediately comes unglued from his objective as he notices how intensely the lady begins searching his eyes and his body - she clearly finds him off-putting, just as everyone else has so far.

Why do I have that effect on people? "No, I do not currently require any assistance. Thank you for your query." With that, Seth continues into the center of the store, looking for any sign of Luna. After a moment or two, he gives up on trying to find her, and turns away to exit the store. That is, until a curtain slides open in the back of the store, revealing a girl with long, black hair and bright, violet eyes.

LUNA! Seth doesn't hesitate to walk right toward her and do the deed he had been intending to do for a long time. He unsheathes his knife, never taking his eyes off of his target. He gets within about ten feet of her before the perky shopkeeper notices him again.

"Sir, I am going to need to ask you to leave - weaponry of any kind is not permitted in the mall."

Seth pauses, and looks down at the unsheathed dagger in his hand.

"That knife, is a weapon. And it is prohibited here. You may either leave the store now or I will have to call security." The woman holds up her cell phone, readying herself to call in reinforcements.

Seth grunts, and clenches his teeth. "You have no business telling me what to do." Before he can take any further steps, the woman blocks his path and presses a panic button. An alarm sounds, and Seth watches as his target locks eyes with him for a split second before shrieking and running out the door with her gaudy pink-striped shopping bag in tow.

Well gee, thanks a lot. Seth shakes his head and rolls his eyes, as he is forced to let Luna get away due to the unwelcome grip of the woman's hand on his arm.

"You're not going *anywhere* until security gets here."

Seth takes one look at her steady gaze, and then in one swift motion, he dislodges his arm from her grip by bending her arm at an odd angle, causing her to scream in pain and let go of him. When she finally does, he bolts right out of the store, running in the direction where he saw Luna go - but he's too late, because she is nowhere to be seen.

CHAPTER 20

"At the mall, you say?" Officer Carnes taps his pen against the deteriorating wood finish on the top of his desk. "You're really sure it was him?" He raises a medium-brown eyebrow as he absorbs the information that is coming to him through the phone. "Okay, okay. Yes, I'll file that as a report. What was he doing again? An assault weapon? Okay, roger that… yeah this kid is bad news, that's for sure. Thanks again, Sanders. Okay, bye now."

He ends the call and starts hastily scribbling down information in a notebook. *This kid has been sighted so many places causing trouble, and yet no one can seem to catch him - very interesting. Little master of disguise, eh? We'll see about that… we'll just have to see.*

✱✱✱

After her shift, Jade goes directly to Evander's pod. *I wonder what he's going to tell me? Hopefully nothing too bad happened since the last meetings - we're just not ready yet. Then again, will we ever be? No, probably not - a revolution of this magnitude just isn't… usual. Or normal. None of this is.* She shakes her head, hoping her worrisome thoughts would dissipate into the fog of the Upperworld - but they don't. They never really do, no matter how hard she tries to focus. Then again, knowing how to operate under pressure is part of her job description - but despite centuries of experience, this is one obstacle that seems much bigger. And that's understandable, because it really is.

She rings the doorbell notifying Evander of her arrival, and he opens the door for her. His tired eyes stare back at her from a sullen face.

"Yes, I am as tired as I look. Come on in, though." Jade closes the door behind her, and clicks it into place, sealing them both in the soundproof dead zone.

"Well, you said you had something important to tell me from your meeting, right? She crosses her arms over her chest, preparing for the worst but hoping for something good, for once.

"Indeed, I think it's a good thing… of course, we'll have to propose it to your group as well, to make sure they're onboard with it…"

"Well, what is it? I don't have all day, you know."

Evander rolls his eyes, and then scratches the back of his head. "They think Onyx would be best as the leader of the Upperworld."

Jade's jaw drops, but slowly nods. There was a small part of her that was hoping *she* would be elected as leader, but granted, it *was* a long shot - even she knew that.

"Oh, okay. Yes, I suppose that would do. What was their reasoning?" She tries to get the information out of him, as if to find out why she herself was slighted. Evander, being as tired as he is, is rendered quite oblivious to her subtle hints.

"Well, he has four centuries of in-depth Earth and humanoid studies under his belt, as well as experience working in the Upperworld, and more recently, on Earth. He's a prime choice because he's seen it all, and that almost guarantees that he would be considered a worthy vessel for the life current to flow through."

Jade chews on her bottom lip and avoids eye contact with Evander. "That's all… very solid. I… cannot think of any reason why not." She allows the new information to wash over her, as the feeling of defeat hitting her like a brick wall - neither sensation is fully present without the other.

"Indeed, I'm surprised I didn't think of it myself sooner. He *is* the most logical choice…"

Jade nods, but her frustration doesn't subside. "Evander?"

He turns his head away from the graphs and charts on his tablet. "Yes?"

"Did you ever think…" She pauses to search for the right words. "…Did you ever consider, that maybe… *I* could do it?"

He freezes mid-database search and turns to face her. "Jade, I mean, I don't know. Not that you aren't amazing, but…"

"But *what*, Evander? What do you possibly have to say to me that I haven't thought of already? Because believe me, I have *seen it all*." Her mouth takes the shape of a vicious sneer, and as if on cue, the temperature of Evander's pod seems to drop considerably.

"Jade, I didn't mean… if you want to, you can present your case to the Disturbers, I just… wanted to fill you in, I had no idea you felt that way. Just please remain democratic about it. What works well enough for The United States of America will work well enough for us."

Jade's face becomes ashen and stone-cold. "Thank you for the update, Evander. I'll be going now." She walks over to the door, planting each step with the pressure of a thousand granite boulders hitting the ground.

"Jade, I apologize if I -"

"Save it."

"Okay, well, uh, see you at the next meeting? Or, uh, I guess you'll meet with your group and I'll meet with mine, since there's limited space…"

Jade just glares at him, her cheeks bright red.

"Bye, Evander." She marches out the door and leaves Evander alone in his pod, wondering what went wrong so quickly.

This is odd... I really had no idea she wanted to be the leader of everything... it's kind of a surreal thought. I know Jade is rather... full of herself, sometimes, so I guess it makes sense. But we've got to think about what would be best not only for the Upperworld, but all of humanity, both present and future. And right now, I have to stay focused on that.

Evander sits dejectedly on the floor for a moment, resting his head in his hands. Suddenly, it feels as if he is hurtling into oblivion - or if not himself, maybe the entire human race. *It's pathetic to think how high the stakes are, and how easy it would be to mess this up, very badly. I cannot let that happen.*

In that moment, he vows to himself to make sure that Onyx is the one chosen. Granted, there is currently no way to communicate with him, since his embedded device has been expelled, but Evander figures he can just transport him back to the Upperworld when they need him, since his essential biological info was saved permanently into the main system.

Onyx will know what to do - and I know the groups will choose wisely.

Then he remembers something he found in his research that might just do the trick. Without getting prematurely excited, he steels himself to focus enough to re-open one of the files that he saved to his tablet from his office. A broad smile creeps across his face as he finds what he needs to ensure that Onyx is the one chosen for the job.

Now I just have to hope that he'll be on board with it - knowing Onyx, I am confident that he will be, once I bring him back here and fill him in on everything.

Evander fights the urge to summon Onyx back to the Upperworld too soon, as he knows full well that he is needed on Earth to protect Luna, and hopefully defeat Seth.

I can't leave him there too much longer, but for now, I will, since he is needed there.

He smiles to himself, thinking about how easy it was to foil Jade's elaborate self-absorbed scheme to obtain the highest possible accolades. But he also knows all too well that things are rarely as simple as they first appear.

CHAPTER 21

"Onyx!" Luna feverishly grabs his hand and sprints out of the store, with Onyx running behind her carrying all their shopping bags. They breeze past the many multi-colored displays of other stores as they run, but it all goes by in a blur. Adrenaline courses through their veins as they both struggle to catch their breath.

"Luna, was it really *that* bad? I mean, it may be a bit awkward but I didn't think -"

Luna finally stops running once they are safely at the other side of the mall. "It's Seth - he was in the store."

"What? Why didn't you say something?" Onyx's eyes widen in a feverish panic.

"I did - I *screamed* and ran, remember?"

"I know, but if I knew, I could've -"

"What?" Luna plants a hand on her hip and flips her long, dark hair out of her eyes.

"I don't know."

Onyx drops the shopping bags momentarily and pulls her close. "I cannot let that happen again. That was… too close of a call…" His breathing intensifies, and he places his lips on hers as Luna responds wholeheartedly.

"Did you… get a good look at him?"

Luna slowly nods. "He… looks like me, doesn't he?"

"I would think so."

Luna bites her lower lip. "It's just… weird. And he had a knife…"

"He had a knife?"

"That's what I saw..."

Onyx breathes in and out slowly, and closes his eyes. *Was he planning to stab her to death?* He struggles to avoid hyperventilating.

"We need to leave, now. He's probably still in this building. Let's go check on our house - I really hope they let us live in it now."

Luna smiles at him, and grabs some of the bags with one hand, and holds onto Onyx's arm with the other. They both walk rapidly to the mall entrance, and make their way back to their housing complex.

"Onyx?"

"Yeah?"

"Do you... think we'll be okay? I feel like... *he* is always following us. That really... upsets me."

"Well, I can promise you that I will do everything I possibly can to protect you. I don't know how our lives are going to turn out - we've already been through a lot more than the average human, but I'm confident that it'll be good. I think that because *you* are good, Luna. Everything about you is just oozing goodness - it's hard to imagine anything terrible happening to someone with such a high-quality sense of morals..."

Onyx looks at Luna to see that she had almost tuned him out, but she is looking directly at the beautiful, mid-afternoon sky. It isn't quite evening yet, but the sky has almost golden haze about it where it is obvious that midday has come and gone.

"So short answer? Yeah, I think we'll be okay." Onyx kisses the top of her head and leads her into the main desk of the condo complex just a few blocks down the street.

"Hello? My name is Onyx, and I'm here to see if the house I had purchased is ready to live in yet."

The same tight-lipped woman from before is behind the desk, this time sporting a spotless-white blouse with a matching beige suit jacket and skirt. Her glasses are poised condescendingly on the bridge of her very long nose.

"Weren't you dressed in a costume before?"

Onyx shakes his head.

"Oh, so you mean you dressed like that normally? *Okay then…*"

Onyx manages to smile politely, even though this woman is insulting him every chance she gets. In a moment like this, he is reminded of the guide who trained him centuries ago and how important it is to treat all people with respect, even when they do not deserve it.

"Typically new buyers are notified via a phone call when their move-in day has been scheduled. Did someone call you yet?"

"I do not have a phone number on file, so I decided to just come check instead."

His rebuttal to the woman's curt reply clearly is making her suspicious of his intent, but she turns to consult her computer anyway.

"Well, Mister Onyx, it *appears* that your home is… ready for you. That is pretty rare, usually the process takes more than a day. Well, *lucky you.*" Her sarcastic slur on those last couple of words are not lost on Onyx's ears - his Earth studies make him privy to different human habits, personalities, and cultures. He does his best not to upset her any further, but her words leave a small sting.

"Here are two house keys, one for you… and your wife. Welcome to Aquatic Springs." She tosses a plastic smile their way, and then goes back to typing away on her computer. Onyx shrugs his shoulders and leads Luna toward their new home.

CHAPTER 22

I was so close, but I lost her - I always do. Seth dejectedly mumbles to himself as he walks around the mall, searching to find Luna again. *I could have done it, I could have really done it. Then I would have completed my mission and could go home.*

Seth mutters some expletives under his breath that he had picked up from his time on Earth so far. Everything about being on Earth worked a lot differently than being in the Upperworld, and even though he hadn't been there very long either, it was his first conscious memory since what he referred to as his "re-awakening". So naturally, he would compare all the oddities of being on Earth to the very different atmosphere of the Upperworld.

He stops for a moment, and realizes that Luna and Onyx likely would have rapidly left the mall upon seeing him there.

What cowards they are! The least they could do is face me and just get it over with - running away is only going to elongate her own suffering. Wouldn't it be easier to just... move on to the next realm? The girl must die... and running from her fate will do nothing to change that.

After a quick perusal of his fewer and fewer options, Seth decides to make his way out of the mall to see if he can find them before they get too far away, and he has to start from square one again. He makes his way past all the brightly-colored store displays, but makes sure to take a detour around the shop where he was almost captured - that would just be another setback, and there is no time for any more setbacks. Her death must happen as soon as possible, lest Zephyr would become upset with him. And having a frustrated boss is no way to start a symbiotic partnership.

Seth continues moving through the mall at a brisk pace, narrowly dodging small children and families walking in the opposite direction. Some of the children cry when they see him - his appearance isn't overly disturbing, but he undoubtedly has a bit of a strange energy about him that certainly gets a significant amount of attention from onlookers.

He quickly gets to the main entrance of the mall, and opens the door into the late-afternoon sunlight. The sky is a deep orange, as evening rapidly approaches. *Well, looks like it'll be another night of sleeping under the stars.* Seth mumbles a few more expletives to himself and makes his way back to the main part of town, where the park and benches are. He's hoping to see Onyx and Luna on the way, but nothing is guaranteed. And the scariest thing is, Seth is beginning to doubt that he'll ever find them at all. Doubt is the one thing that Seth is not programmed to know how to fight. The parasitic emotion quickly begins to burrow into his inner core, tearing away his resolve by the shreds and eating away at his confidence. He tries to shake it off, but to no avail.

Well, maybe I'll have better luck tomorrow after I get some... sleep. I think that's what people call temporary unconsciousness here. In the meantime, I'll keep my eyes open for Onyx and Luna... even if I have to kill him to get to her.

***

"Settle down, everyone. We're about to start - thank you, thank you." Jade tries to grab the attention of the various sorters, guides, orderlies, record keepers, and technicians in her pod as she commences session one of the meeting of the Disturbers. The crowds had gotten so large, that due to limited space, her and Evander decided to do multiple sessions so that everyone could fit in at some point and get the information and updates they need. Although, that conversation happened *before* their fight, which left them both feeling both frustrated and drained. Regardless of any of their personal feelings, the importance of their work vastly outweighs it. They know they must stay focused on what is really important: rallying the Disturbers together and appointing a replacement for Zephyr before he becomes completely obsolete.

"As you may know, Zephyr is getting weaker and weaker every day." The crowd answers back in an excited chorus, pumping their fists in the air and cheering.

"Yes, it is exciting how close we are getting to putting this plan into action, but before we can do so, there is a matter of utter importance to attend to first." She pauses for a moment before beginning the speech she had meticulously prepared beforehand.

“Evander has told me that he has spoken with his sector of the coalition, and that they have technically all decided on a new leader.”

The crowd erupts in questioning murmurs. “Who is it? What’d they decide?” One of the younger sorters yells from her spot near Jade’s water cooler.

“Well, this suggestion to me, seems extremely improbable - you see, they chose someone… who not only has not been here in a while, but also has a history of getting caught up in human-like emotions, and making snap decisions because of that. Do those things sound like sufficient qualifications to lead not only the entire Upperworld, but the entire human race, present *and* future?”

The crowd murmurs some more, and some of the bolder ones yell angrily, some even resorting to expletives that they likely learned through their human studies courses.

“That’s what I thought - I agree with you there. I should tell you, if you haven’t figured it out yet… the candidate in question… is Onyx.”

At the exact moment she utters his name, the crowd explodes with anger, distaste, and shock:

“He’s not our leader!”

“Why would they want him?”

“He’s part humanoid, that’s just not natural…”

“There’s no way he’s cut out for this.”

“Jade, what are we going to do?”

A small, devious smile threatens to emote on Jade's lips, but she keeps it under wraps in order to maintain her professional position of leadership.

"Well, there's no need to fret... because there *is* another option..."

An excited murmur is heard over the crowd, but they quickly quiet down to find out who the alternative is.

"Me. I am eligible to be the leader. I hereby nominate myself for the highest position of prestige in the Upperworld - that of Most High Being."

The crowd of Upperworld beings is completely silent for what feels like a small eternity, and then a slow rumbling can be felt as they all begin to clap, very slowly. It begins with just Brielle, the petite sorter in the back row clapping, and then they all follow suit, all the way from Vidia to the eldest record keeper, Brahms. It is fortunate that the entire pod has been soundproofed and converted into a dead zone, because the noise emitted by all the excited beings would be enough to cause quite a stir, if it was audible from outside Jade's habitation pod.

"Jade, you are perfect for the job!"

"This is a magnanimous step in the right direction..."

"We can trust her, I think anyone could."

"I have absolutely no doubt that she can handle it."

Jade grins widely as the accolades continue. "I am most delighted to hear that I have your support. The only problem lies in the fact that the others will likely still be pulling for Onyx. We *must* stay the course, and remain focused no matter what."

The entire pod erupts in an empowered chorus, and Jade smiles gleefully in the low lamplight. *And so it begins.*

VOLUME TWO:
THE REVOLUTION

CHAPTER 1

Zephyr lays dejectedly on his throne, the current fighting to flow through him - the connection is rapidly weakening. Barely able to keep his eyes open, his eyelids flutter a bit, his body limp as a rag doll. The fog of the Upperworld seems to react to his weakening life essence, as it seems to dissipate around him. Overhead, the luminescent lighting blinks ominously, likely a precursor to the disasters to come.

"Excuse me, Most High Being?"

Zephyr manages to open one cavernous, dark eye to find out who is looking to get his attention.

"Speak."

The orderly opens her mouth to speak, but hesitates. She knows full well that her news will greatly upset him, and it isn't clear what he is going to do about it.

"Well, I don't know how to say this…"

"You must try. Time is running out."

"What? What do you mean by that?"

Zephyr visibly tenses, and an uncomfortable grimace spreads over his ghastly face.

"That is none of your concern. Now speak."

The orderly shifts uncomfortably from foot to foot, and bides her time looking for just the right words.

"Well, you see, I've heard… murmurings…"

Zephyr's flaming hair glows a bit brighter at this remark. "Of what?"

The orderly swallows her own saliva nervously. "… an uprising… they - some of them… want to revolt."

Zephyr is dejectedly sprawled out on his throne, exceptionally weak at this point, and yet, he still reacts to what he is hearing as the orderly shifts her weight nervously in front of him.

"What are you talking about?"

"I… I heard… some of my fellow Upperworld beings discussing some secret meetings and efforts to dethrone you."

Zephyr's cavernous, dark, menacing eyes become even deeper as he takes in the information provided for him by the small girl.

"That is UNACCEPTABLE. I will not allow… this to occur." Zephyr clearly wants to raise his fist in frustration, but he is so weak at this point, that he cannot even sit up straight without assistance, so he just lays back and breathes heavily in disgust instead. His large, macabre visage casts shadows over the already-darkened Grand Hall, and the orderly cowers in his imposing presence.

The orderly nods. "I figured you had a right to know, Most High Being."

"Who is behind this?"

"Well, some of the orderlies are part of the coalition, as well as some of the sorters, record keepers, and guides. I am one of the few that are still on your side, Most High One. They are growing in number rapidly, and it is hard to contain them."

He sits vulnerably on his throne, awaiting further explanation from the orderly.

"Well, young one, I applaud your honesty and loyalty. For that, you shall be rewarded. In the mean time, please try to stifle anyone who is part of this, and I will see what can be done."

✳✳✳

"I don't know what you have heard about the procedures, but there is some unrest happening amongst us, and that cannot continue. As the sixteenth president of the United States so wisely proclaimed many years ago - 'A divided house cannot stand.'" Evander stands at the front of the meeting of all the Disturbers for the first time ever - there are so many of them now that he had to rig the biggest lecture hall with soundproofing to accommodate all of them at once. He is now using the few moments he has before Jade arrives to speak to everyone all at once without her getting in the way - a precious opportunity that he dares not waste.

"What's going on here?" Jade storms into the room in a huff with her coarse, silver hair tied up into a militant bun, and her typically immaculate clothing without a single wrinkle.

Evander looks over to the crowd hesitantly, hoping that Jade would not undermine the small amount of authority he did have, as well as come to her senses about how ridiculously mistaken she would be to try to be the Most High Being.

"Well, I am currently explaining to our loyal followers that there has been some significant discord within, and that we cannot be successful if we do not cast away our differences - starting now."

Jade lets out a hearty laugh. "Fine. But you do realize that votes still have to be cast - as you have said, democracy is always the best way to go. If it's good enough for America, then it is certainly good enough for us."

Evander steels himself against her powerful gaze, as well as the chaos exploding in the audience. Everyone is arguing with one another, and it quickly becomes all too apparent that nothing will be accomplished until this disagreement is rectified.

"Well, to accommodate this *setback*, I have produced a ballot for your consideration. Please pass these around, and sign your name to each one. Check here if you believe, as I do, that Onyx is the best and only choice for leadership-"

"- Or check here if you believe, as you should, that I am the best candidate for the job" Jade intercepts his speech while pointing a resolute finger at the space on the ballot that her name takes up. Her intense glare meets the eyes of many in the crowd, ensuring that whether or not they want her to lead, they just might vote for her solely out of fear.

Evander runs a hand through his hair as he always does when he gets stressed. "All our fate, is up to you all. I will run each ballot through a digital counting system so that the final count is impartial and fair. But bear in mind, everyone, something that you should know…"

All eyes land on Evander as he readies himself to say the one thing that he honestly believes can sway all their votes in the right direction.

"After doing some research on the qualifications and requirements for a Most High Being to survive the transference of the life-current that flows through them, they require a body that has some tie to Earth, so that the current will take to it."

"Wait, so Zephyr has a tie to Earth?" One of the younger sorters pipes in with the question likely on everyone's mind.

Evander pauses for a moment to mentally recall what he had learned through his research before answering. "Yes, but only because he was appointed to this position by the council of the gods at the dawn of existence – he's been doing this quite literally since time itself began."

The young sorter nods, but many questions still seem to float just behind her eyes – but those would have to wait for the time being. "Well, no wonder he's quite worn out at this point."

"Okay but what does that have to do with Onyx?" Jade files one of her stubborn hangnails while only half-listening to Evander's political pitch. She has no idea that his next words would be the final nails in the coffin of her nefarious plans.

"Onyx has a permanent tie to Earth, since his essence was originally meant as a humanoid."

"So?" Jade spits the word out of her mouth as a dart aimed at a target, even though her confidence is beginning to slightly waver.

"So… do you have any ties to Earth? For your sake, I hope you do. Because if you don't, the moment you sit on that throne, the current will obliterate you."

A collective gasp fills the large room.

"Well, I, uh…"

"That's what I figured. The Upperworld is all you've ever known - you're just not cut out for this, and now it appears that you are physically incapable of the job, even though you want it."

Jade blushes, and smiles as the embarrassment of her own inadequacy fills her face. The crowd grows silent, but some of the original Jade supporters continue to whoop and holler, clearly not understanding the magnitude of the situation:

"Onyx may have a tie to Earth, but he isn't cut out for this!"

"That guy is a joke."

"There's no way he can hack this!"

"I *will not* let the entirety of humanity fall into his hands!"

"He's far too emotional to assign souls into lives - think about what could happen!"

Evander sighs at their obvious imbecility.

"I still believe in democracy, and I can see that there is still some unrest. So, we will still collect the ballots, just to keep things fair." He rolls his eyes and just hopes that they will come to their senses before it is too late.

CHAPTER 2

"Well, here we are…" Onyx opens the door to their condo and pauses to breathe, relishing the fact that they are finally safe. Having a home where they can lock out the terrors of the outside world - like Seth - is a welcome reprieve. The darkness of the early night sky fills the windows, so he flicks on the main light switch to better see everything.

"It's… perfect, Onyx." Luna smiles at him as she settles herself on a nearby couch. "So, this is where our lives will take place, right?"

Onyx grins and then puts all their shopping bags by the front door as he momentarily allows himself to sink into the plush cushioning of the couch. After a long day, he is exhausted and his feet are beginning to feel the effects of all the walking.

"Tomorrow, we should look into buying a motorized vehicle to get around in. I can't walk around everywhere, I'm just not used to it."

"Do you - we, have money for that?"

Onyx nods. "I can continue to use the Earth-bound Upperworld bank account until I find a job. So yes, we have money for it."

"You always know just what to say…" Luna scoots closer to Onyx and cuddles with him on the couch for a moment, laying her head on his shoulder and draping her legs across his. He gently pats her shoulder and then breaks the embrace.

"I, uh, I'll take the clothes and supplies upstairs. Also, you should get ready to go to sleep, it's getting late and we've had a long day."

Luna opens her mouth to speak, but Onyx disappears up the stairs before she can say a word. She immediately follows him, and walks into a bedroom where he is hastily folding and putting away their new clothes.

"Here are some clothes suitable for sleeping." He hands her a comfortable pair of sweatpants and a tee shirt, and then turns back to the folding. For some odd reason, Luna notices that Onyx suddenly seems very tense.

"Onyx, is something wrong?"

He pauses his folding for a moment, and looks at her with his bright cerulean irises. "No, why would you think that?"

"Well, you seem tense, and you aren't looking me in the eye…"

Onyx exhales, and realizes that she is absolutely right. "I suppose I am a bit tense, Luna. I'm sorry, I didn't mean to worry you. I think, I just…" He pauses to find just the right words. "Earlier today, I was so frightened at the prospect of how close I was to losing you to Seth in that store - I honestly had no idea he was that close until it was almost too late. If something happened to you on my watch, I don't know - "

Luna cuts off the rest of that terrible prospect by firmly placing her lips on his, and he heartily reciprocates. He immediately drops the shirt he was folding and places his hands around her waist, pulling her as close to himself as possible. Their body temperatures begin to steadily rise, as the kiss deepens, and their two heartbeats synchronize as one. Without missing a beat, Luna's hands begin to wander all over Onyx's trim, muscular torso, calmly noticing the warmth of his skin under her trembling palms. He feels her hands move to the small of his back and under the hem of his shirt, and takes the subtle cue. Onyx gently carries her over to his bed, and eases himself over her, allowing the most visceral and human desires embedded in his very essence to take over. In the following moments, he allows himself the opportunity to indulge in the most desperate desire he has ever had - to show her how much he truly loves her, and always has, through time and space. The skin of their bodies compliments each other seamlessly as they join together. Their connection and needs are stronger than all of the things they have fought through, because they never forgot what could have been. He knows how Luna has suffered, and ever-so-gently ensures that he does not impose himself on her in any way. But she is his, and he is hers. And now, as they finally become one, the way they were always meant to, the world around them sings, as the stars outside their window sparkle with the gleam of a million diamonds.

✳✳✳

The morning sun rises, illuminating Seth's dark frame sprawled out on the park bench. He opens one eye, and then the other, regretting his unwanted return to consciousness. The pressure of finding and ultimately killing Luna is beginning to get to him, and sleep is a seductive mistress.

His limbs are sore, yet again, from lying on the hard, cold, slightly damp surface.

I just have to keep walking... and searching. They are bound to be somewhere nearby... just keep moving.

Without a better option, he resorts to aimlessly walking down the street, hoping to either find Luna, or a clue that would lead him to her. He knows all too well that Zephyr is probably becoming quite upset with him for faltering in his approach to carry out the deed.

It has to be done, and soon. When I see her, I'll slit her throat and worry about logistics later. That is the only way.

A devilish smile oozes across his face at the thought of Luna's frail, lifeless body laying limp on the ground, and a gushing stream of blood gushing through the gash in her neck like a geyser. He'd hit the major artery on the first try, and then hopefully return to the Upperworld to claim his place of honor as Zephyr's right-hand confidant with a simple press of the black pendant.

It will happen, it is just a matter of when.

***

"Gotcha, Officer Carnes. I'll secure the perimeter, and if I see the peculiar character in the blue jumpsuit, as you had described, I will be sure to bring him right in for questioning on the grounds of local discomfort and security."

Officer Phil Jones reattaches his cellphone to his utility belt and continues walking past the park, towards the downtown area where the diner is - he needs to get his daily fill of homemade donuts and coffee. And that's when he sees a rather sketchy, incriminating figure in a blue jumpsuit walking down the street.

"Hey! Hey you, I need to speak with you. Now!" Officer Jones starts jogging toward Seth, but one glance at the officer is all it takes for him to sprint down the street away from him. Within seconds, the two enter into a mad chase, and Seth's heart nearly beats out of his chest as the adrenaline rushes through his veins. As the officer begins to gain on him, Seth takes a rapid turn down a side street and continues forcing his body to move faster than it really can comfortably.

Right, left, right, left.... breathe....

He brushes some loose strands of his jet-black dark hair out of his face as sweat drips down his hairline. The sun is already beating down significantly in the mid-morning hours, and he can feel his body becoming fatigued, from both the rising environmental temperatures and the intense pressure on his bones as he pounds his feet into the concrete. After a few agonizing moments of pure desperation, Seth's gaze lands on a nearby shed where he can hide from the police officer.

Great, I can hide there!

He enters the space and immediately shuts the door, hoping that the policeman didn't see where he went past the sharp corner he took. As Seth catches his breath, he allows himself to slump down next to a nearby wall, where he counts the blissful moments away from the eyes of the world. It has been so long since he has been freed from the prying eyes of curious humans who keep threatening him, or making him feel the need to threaten them back.

Once he finally regulates his breathing and pulse, Seth regroups and tries to think about where Luna might be. He absentmindedly glances around the shed he took refuge in, and all he sees are various gardening tools, bare wood slats, and the shards of light breaking through them from the mid-morning sun.

Nothing catches his eye until something does - on the very wall he is leaning against is a bit of long, dark hair caught on a nail. *Someone else had been sitting here too.* He gently pulls a piece of hair from the nail it was tangled against and holds it to his face, sniffing it vigorously to detect a possible scent. To his utter delight, he recognizes it as Luna's hair. As animalistic qualities go, Seth has a very keen sense of smell, not unlike a wolf or some other powerful, wild animal. And at this moment, it has served him very well.

Luna... Luna was here... He breathes a sigh of relief and begins to grin and laugh uncontrollably. Then his eyes shift to a small piece of card stock paper on the floor - he wastes no time in examining that as well.

Aquatic Springs Condominiums? I'm thinking that might be the next best place to check for Luna.

CHAPTER 3

Zephyr is incredibly weak now, that his entire body limp on his throne, and his face motionless. The life-force current is still flowing through him, but only at the rate of a trickle. The end is soon, and he knows it. But he also knows that there is an uprising occurring, and that something must be done about it before time runs out and he is overthrown. That is why he set a counter-plan in motion to try to keep the ruffians at bay.

"Jewel… did you… did you handle it?"

One of the many orderlies approaches his throne in the Grand Hall, and meekly curtsies.

"Yes, Most High Being. I have set the plan in motion. It is only a matter of time now before the revolutionists realize that they are being watched, realize their efforts are futile, and then cease plotting against you."

Zephyr is hardly able to move, but a slow, slight nod from his chin tells Jewel that he understands and approves.

"That is… good to hear."

She nods respectfully.

"Is there anything I can do for you, Zephyr? Anything at all, perhaps some more ambrosia to dull the pain?"

Zephyr groans in protest.

"I know you don't like it, but you're very weak now and it might strengthen you."

Again, another slow nod from Zephyr tells her to proceed.

"Okay, I will be right back with it."

The atmosphere of the Upperworld has adapted to the change in Zephyr's energy, and all processes are beginning to feel the pinch. As the life-force energy begins to slowly seep out of his limp body, with some even hitting the floor, and promptly evaporating, the defects will begin to manifest themselves.

Any moment, any time now, human history will begin to collapse, and all the Upperworld beings will be dragged down into the depths of the Underworld. Their nearly perpetual bond to Zephyr is undeniable, and in the grand scheme of things, it will be fatal for all beings, both mortal and yes - even the immortal, as immortality is not immune to the wiles of a depreciating leader.

Only time will tell how much time is left - and once it is revealed, it will be too late.

***

After what feels like a small eternity of collecting the ballots, Evander begins to have the digital counting system tally up the ballots in plain sight of everyone in accordance, so that no one can question the accuracy of the results once they are revealed. He is about to press the button to finalize the process when a bit of unrest echoes through the crowd.

"What? What's going on?" Evander pauses mid-process and crosses his arms, clearly irritated.

"There's a... camera in here." Griffin shrugs his shoulders and looks at Evander to get his attention.

"Oh, absolutely not. I've de-bugged and silenced everything in this room, there is no possible way -"

"Just look!"

Evander makes his way over to where Griffin and some others are standing and point up at the ceiling. And low and behold, there indeed *is* a small, round, black sensor with just one, solitary red light blinking rhythmically about every three seconds, as measured on Earth.

"That... that cannot be here. Everyone, quiet! This has to be attended to before we can continue."

"But the voting!"

"Yeah! Who won?"

"We need to know!"

"This cannot wait!"

"Silence!" Evander's interjection reverberates through the large discussion room which is currently housing all the Disturbers in one of their usual strategy meetings. "We have to be careful, *they* may know things now." With a finger to his lips, Evander pulls a step ladder and a small hammer out of a nearby closet, and the crowd watches as he quickly scales the structure and reaches up to the incriminating sensor. With three quick, forceful hits, Evander tries to simultaneously dislodge and destroy the sensor, which could be picking up their dialogue, and therefore, their plans.

"It's not… it's not breaking." Evander scratches his head as the small hairs on the back of his neck begin to stand on end in a panic.

"What do you mean it's not? Let me at it."

Evander climbs down from the ladder and hands Jade the hammer, hoping that maybe she would be able to break it. When she reaches the top of the ladder, the hammer makes contact with the sensor, sending sparks everywhere, and the beings in the crowd move as far away from the area as possible, squishing uncomfortably to the sides of the room. Jade hits it again, and again, and again, but to no avail - the sensor is left without even so much as a scratch.

"It's not, it can't be…" Jade's eyes widen as Evander nods at her from his vantage point at the base of the ladder.

"Oh but it is… that sensor is *indestructible*, and there could be countless other ones. They've been installed because… they're on to us."

"What? Who is on to us?" One of the sorters raises a hand, and the record keeper standing next to her nods his head, clearly thinking the same thing.

"Well, very possibly, Zephyr has gotten wind of our… plans."

"Shhhh! Isn't that still transmitting?" Jade interrupts Evander to remind him of their newly-discovered security breach.

"Very likely, yes. But honestly, since there isn't anything we can do about it, we need to just continue on, now more importantly than ever. Now that it may be implicitly clear what we are planning to do, we may need to put our plan into action even *sooner* than we had originally thought."

Discomfort and fear spreads through the crowd like wildfire as everyone begins to panic.

"Yes, I understand that this is all very scary, but it is of utmost importance that we stay strong. Fear is our biggest weakness, and to win this, to really, really win this, I am going to need your continued support."

Many heads nod as Evander continues to process the ballots through the digitized machine.

"Okay, ready for your results?"

After a few moments of sheer and utterly desperate anticipation, Evander takes a deep breath.

"After putting your ballots through this secure, digitized counter, the new leader of the Upperworld, in charge of generating new beings and placing existing ones into their appropriate lives is…"

As everyone gasps, the screen shows a name that some had grown to dislike:

Onyx.

CHAPTER 4

The mid-morning sun reaches through the window of Luna and Onyx's bedroom and gently wakes them from a long night of blissful love and a deep, well-deserved sleep. Her long, dark hair is draped over Onyx's shoulder, while he holds her close in his muscular arm. Tangled in the bed sheets, sleep slowly melts away as the light in the room becomes steadily brighter and more pronounced. Onyx groans quietly as the sun hits his still-tired eyelids, but he quickly comes to and remembers that they are safe and happy - at least for now. And after all that they've been through, that is quite worth celebrating. He presses his lips to Luna's forehead.

"Good morning, Luna…" The whispered words tickle her ear, and she wakes up to find herself in Onyx's passionate embrace. Her eyelids flutter open, and she meets his loving gaze.

He kisses her again, passionately, and wraps his arm around her, making the tiny hairs on her neck and bare back stand up from the electricity he sends through her.

"You're so… beautiful, Luna…"

She inhales softly, breathing in his natural scent and reveling the feel of his embrace. "Onyx, what is 'beautiful'?" He pauses for a moment, realizing for the first time in a while that Luna hasn't had all the extensive culture and assimilation training that he has had, and therefore will not necessarily grasp every colloquial term that she comes across.

"Well, it's... you! You are... aesthetically pleasing, to me. So you're beautiful. It's a good thing - you are perfect." He places a quick, chaste kiss on her lips once more before hastily getting up to get dressed and begin the day.

"There is much to do today, you'd better get up and prepare."

Luna sits up in bed, the sheets pulled up around her shoulders. "Prepare for what?"

"More assimilation, and some more logistical needs must be met." Onyx struggles to pull a pair of jeans over his feet. "My pod, what in the world do they make these things out of? I can barely fit them over my feet!"

Luna giggles at his battle with the denim pants, and just sits in bed watching him for a few more minutes.

"What?"

"*You're* beautiful too."

Onyx opens his mouth to explain the gender-related connotations surrounding certain words and phrases on Earth, but he stops himself, realizing that it just isn't important enough to ruin the moment with that kind of arbitrary nit picking.

"Well, thank you!" He smiles back at her, and then grabs some of his new clothes from the dresser.

"But you've really got to get dressed. There is much to do before the light is gone for the day!"

Luna sighs. "I just... don't want this to end."

"What exactly don't you want to end?"

She pauses for a moment, trying to fit her complex thoughts and emotions into more concise sentences. "Well, this - everything… here. You, me, together… this home, this comfy bed. And we're safe - for the first time in what feels like forever, we're not running away or living in fear."

Onyx pauses while running a comb through his short, icy blonde hair. "Well, we cannot stay here forever…"

Luna shrugs her shoulders, letting one side of the bed sheet sag slightly lower than the other. "And why not?"

Onyx smiles at her, considering her to be joking, but when she does not return an equally-amused grin, he realizes a potential discrepancy in her mindset.

"Well, we have been given a chance at a wonderful life on Earth - we cannot afford to waste that."

"But, but… Seth…" Luna's eyes begin to tear up, and she burrows down back under the covers. The fear of the unknown, outside of those doors, is enough to keep her inside potentially forever.

"Seth cannot hurt you because I won't allow him to." Onyx walks over to the nervous mound of blankets and pillows that have consumed Luna's frail, petite frame.

"But what are you going to do?"

"Do when?"

"When we see him? He *is* going to find us eventually - what are you going to do when he does?"

Onyx runs a hand through his freshly combed hair. "I'll protect you, that's what. At any cost, I will ensure that you, Luna, are utterly and completely safe."

A sigh is audible from underneath the blanket. "But what are you going *to do*? You can't just run away every time… what if, what if you have to fight him?"

Onyx freezes mid-thought, as he realizes the depth of her logic, and how uncomfortably right she is.

"I… I wasn't trained for hand-to-hand combat. But I will do my best." He awkwardly pats her back through the blanket and makes his way to the bathroom across the hall. A few sharp inhales move down his throat, and a feeling of light-headedness descends upon him like a heavy fog after the rain.

I'd like to think I'd be able to take him in a fight... but I really doubt that I can. He's not... as weak as he looks. Seth is smart, quick on his feet, and has a powerful intellect. There's no guarantee that I'll come out of this alive... and if I don't, neither will Luna.

CHAPTER 5

Peeking through the small gap in the door of the shed to make sure that the police officer that was chasing him gave up, Seth opens the door quietly and walks toward the main street. After being spotted before, he is extra vigilant this time to ensure that he is not being watched or followed. As he walks in a general direction down the main street, he comes to the harsh realization that he has no idea where to find Aquatic Springs Condominiums.

It must be nearby, but I'm not totally sure how nearby. Or exactly where.

He shifts his gaze to a young couple sitting nearby on a park bench, enjoying some late-morning coffee.

Maybe I can ask them. They are probably local dwellers and will know the area.

He wastes no time strategizing any further than that, and walks straight toward them. The girl meets his eyes from yards away, and understandably begins to tense up, clutching the arm of the boy she is with. Her long, dark, curly brown hair blows in the slight breeze, and the boy next to her runs his hand through his own curly dirty-blonde hair. She whispers something in his ear, and he makes eye contact with Seth as he approaches them. As soon as his eyes meet Seth's, he stiffens as if an electric current shot through him - and recognition floods his face.

When Seth reaches them, he stops only a few feet in front of them, clearly not familiar with instinctual notions of personal space.

"Uh, can I help you?" The nappy-headed boy asks his question with much concern in his voice as the girl next to him stares off into the distance, likely to avoid eye contact with the mysterious figure.

"Do you know where *Aquatic Springs Condominiums* is located?"

The boy shifts his weight uncomfortably. "That depends - who's asking?"

"My name is Seth."

Recognition flashes across his face momentarily, and then dissipates, as his muscles flinch, readying for defense if the need arises.

"Seth? Uh, I don't know anyone by that name, I'm not sure if I should tell you anything."

"It is okay, I do not know you either." Seth gingerly grips the hilt of the dagger in his pocket, readying it to be used at any moment.

"So why are you asking me then?"

"It was my assumption that you live around this local area, and would therefore know if it was nearby." He grips the dagger a bit tighter, waiting for just the precise moment.

The girl next to him squirms uncomfortably on the bench. *"Just tell him, Anthony."*

He turns to her in disbelief as Seth anxiously waits. *"But I think that's..."*

"It doesn't matter. Just go ahead. He creeps me out." She gives his hand a quick squeeze and looks up at Seth.

"Well, okay. Yeah that's... near here. It's, um, down the street that way, a bit. You can't miss it, just look for the fountain with the large fish statue in it."

The grip on the dagger releases.

Seth nods. "Your assistance is much appreciated." A sneer spreads across his face as he abruptly turns on his heel and begins to move in the other direction. Anthony and his girlfriend watch as his bony, articulated frame marches back the way it came. His deliberate footsteps crush every blade of grass they come into contact with, leaving a trail of flattened greenery in their wake.

"So you said you... know that guy?"

Anthony turns to face his girlfriend.

"He just... his eyes... reminded me of someone."

"Oh my gosh, don't tell me you're still hung up on that girl Luna again, are you?" She crosses her arms in protest and deliberately looks off into the distance now, not as a distraction, but as a defense.

"No, look, Miranda, I already told you, it's not... like that. She was someone I was caring for until her... guardian came for her, that's all. Just being a good samaritan, I promise that really was it. I didn't mean to upset you, but I think that guy... had her eyes."

She reluctantly meets his gaze. "What do you mean he 'had her eyes'? Did he pluck them out of her head?"

Anthony gulps. "It's uh, a *really* long story. And I don't even fully understand all of it."

"Well are you gonna tell me or not?"

He runs his hand through his hair once more. "I mean, I've got nothing to hide, if that's what you're worried about. It was before you and I got together, so it doesn't matter."

She exhales, but some tension remains in her throat. "I know, I just…"

Reaching for his hand, she searches for the right words to explain how she is feeling. "I wish I knew you sooner, and I feel like I missed out on your life so far. So sometimes, I think I ask a lot about you because it's like a futile attempt to catch up, you know? Like, do you ever feel like I was *supposed* to know you sooner, but for some odd reason I just didn't?"

Anthony smiles at her, and leans in to place a quick kiss on her lips. She kisses him back, but he pulls away so he can say what he needs to before the intoxication kicks in and he completely forgets. "I absolutely relate to what you're saying. It's very true that I often feel like something was… missing, with us. Maybe it's lost time, or some kind of freaky time warp messed up fate. But whatever it is, I am so incredibly happy… that I have you now."

He puts his arm around her shoulder, pulling her close, and stares off into the distance. He sips his coffee with his free hand, and inhales deeply, enjoying the clean, fresh air, and Miranda's subtle, fruity perfume.

"It's comforting to know that at least we're on the same page, even if it seems like it took forever to get here."

"Totally."

“So that freak in the blue, rubbery suit?”

Anthony sighs. “I mean, to be honest, it was implied through all the craziness that he was related to her somehow, but she never really explained it to me. That’s pretty much all I’ve got.”

She nods, but a question still remains behind her eyes. “Okay, but why is he so… odd? Off-putting? Weird? It’s like he’s not… from this planet - what a freak.”

Anthony smirks. “Well, I guess he’s just… eccentric. I don’t know - now you know as much as I do.”

“Yeah?”

“Yeah.”

CHAPTER 6

"Onyx? Why does it have to be Onyx?" Jade fumes and begins clenching her fists as the crowd begins to hum with wild excitement and anticipation in the aftermath of the voting results.

"Well, that's what the popular vote dictated. You understand that it's only fair to - "

"But he's not even here! He's still on Earth with that ridiculous character who started this whole mess."

Evander swallows back some inflammatory words and tries to figure out the best way to calm down Jade.

"Look, I understand that a lot has happened, but it isn't fair to blame Luna - she is braver than most other sorters would be, especially after such a short time of existing! And Onyx has proven, time and time again, that he is the best one for the job. He is strong, well-studied and…"

"Still stuck on Earth." Jade crosses her arms as her face begins to turn an angry shade of red. "I really believe I can do this, you've got to give me a chance."

Evander shakes his head. "Everyone has spoken! As soon as I determine it to be safe, I'll summon Onyx back to the Upperworld, and the revolution will begin."

Most of the crowd cheers at this exclamation, and Jade offers an explicit hand gesture to everyone else as she stomps out of the large conference room.

"You'll regret this, you really will. See you all in the Underworld, because that's where we're all going to end up!" She slams the door shut behind her, leaving Evander with the crowd of disturbers, ready to plan their next step in this long battle that is about to come to a head.

"Okay, well, she clearly has made her feelings obvious, but we don't need to let that stop us. Please know that I am completely devoted to this cause, and I will ensure that everything goes exactly as planned."

Evander looks out over the audience, and he notices a small hand raised toward the center of the crowd. "Yes? Do you have a question?"

A red-haired sorter lowers her hand and hesitates to speak.

"Well, go on, we haven't got a lot of time, you know."

"I was wondering, what exactly *is* the plan? I know we're going to take down Zephyr and all that, but how exactly are we going to pull that off?"

A smile erupts over Evander's face. "Well, it's a good thing you asked that, since I do believe that I haven't been all that clear about it. If you'll take a look at this map…"

Evander directs his laser pointer toward the holograph presentation that is now floating in front of the crowd.

"This is how it's going to go down…"

***

Luna reluctantly gets out of bed while trying not to trip over their discarded outfits from last night, and walks over to the drawer where Onyx stashed her new clothing that they bought yesterday. Picking through it gingerly, she settles on some fitted black pants, a white shirt, and the deep purple sweater that Onyx liked on her in the store. He said it matched her eyes, and upon looking herself over in the mirror, she can see that it indeed does. She walks out of their bedroom and toward the bathroom, where Onyx is brushing his teeth.

"What are you doing?" Luna looks at him expectantly, and he smiles through the froth that has collected at his lips. He leans over the sink and spits the frothy, white liquid out of his mouth, letting it swirl down the drain.

"I was brushing my teeth - you should do the same."

"What?"

Onyx sighs to himself, realizing how many basic things he'll have to teach Luna about living on Earth. His studies over a few centuries had taught him well, but she hasn't had those opportunities to learn about the world and how to live in it.

"You'll have to remember that we've been relegated to humanoid forms now, which means that these bodies require certain levels of upkeep, maintenance, and routine cleansing." He pauses to grab a fresh toothbrush from one of the bathroom drawers, and then squirts some toothpaste onto it. “Just use this to scrub your teeth, and then spit it out into the sink when you’re done.”

Luna hesitantly takes it from him, and does as she is told. But the sharp minty flavor makes her cough and sputter a bit.

“That’s so weird.”

Onyx smiles at her innocence. “You’ll get used to it, I promise!”

She manages to smile back at him through the frothy liquid, and some of it pools at the corners of her mouth and threatens to cascade off of her lips.

“Okay, now spit it out.”

Luna does as she’s told, but not as Onyx had likely expected.

“I did say ‘into the sink’.”

Luna shrugs her shoulders. “Oops, sorry.”

Onyx smiles sheepishly and shakes his head. “Nothing some paper towels and water can’t clean up.”

Luna brushes her long, dark hair out of her face as Onyx cleans up the mess she accidentally made with the frothy, minty toothpaste.

“You’ll get used to it, I promise. I know… being here, isn’t easy for you.”

Luna shakes her head. “It’s… okay. Difficult, but okay.”

Onyx finishes with his own morning routine, and then heads back to their room to prepare to leave for the day.

“Onyx?”

Luna pokes her head into the room as Onyx places a wad of Earth currency into the front pocket of his new jeans.

"Yes, Luna?"

"I have a question."

"Ask anything."

"What's… this?" She motions between them with her hand, clearly questioning their relationship. "Uh, you're here, and you've helped me so much, and you're taking care of me, and then… last night… what are we?"

At the mention of the previous evening, Onyx blushes, and then turns to meet her gaze.

"I never explained everything to you, did I?"

Luna shakes her head, with a quizzical look on her face. "I guess not."

"Come sit." He pats a place on the still-disheveled bed next to him.

"So, you understand about what happened in the Upperworld, right? How there was a terrible mistake, and you covered for Delphine? I was worried about you - so, so worried about you. And then, I was told something especially shocking. I guess I kept meaning to tell you but I kept putting it off because of everything that was happening. Can you believe this is the first time in forever we haven't been running away from something?"

Luna nods her head. "It has been really scary."

"I know! Which is why I neglected to properly explain everything. In the heat of the moment, other things just seemed more of a pressing need."

"I understand. Continue, please."

Onyx wraps his arm around her petite shoulders, pulling her closer to him.

"Well, it turns out, that you and I weren't originally meant to be sorters."

Luna's back stiffens and she turns to him incredulously. "What? How?"

Onyx pulls her close again, stroking her back to calm her down. "Well, as you very well know at this point, humanoids often do not conduct themselves the way we plan for them to."

Luna nods and shrugs. "Of course, I understand, but what does that have to do with -"

"I was aborted."

"What?"

Onyx takes a deep breath and tries to steady himself before explaining the painful truth of his own existence that he now must carry with him.

"I was supposed to be a humanoid. My Earth mother, she chose to… destroy me before I could be born…" Onyx chokes a little as the words fall out of his mouth. "Zephyr arranged for my soul to be re-absorbed into the Upperworld to give me a chance to live as a sorter. Made sense at the time, I suppose. But it still makes me sick to think about - because there are probably so many others, and they have no idea."

"I'm so confused…"

"I know, it really is a lot to take in."

"But, what does this have to do with me?"

Onyx continues rubbing her back as he tries to find the right way to explain the shocking truth of her own alternate existence.

"Well, do you remember how in the Sorting Room, we decided who lives where and who they end up with as their significant other and life partner?"

Luna nods.

"Well, you were… meant to be mine."

"What?"

"I know, it's shocking, but you were also meant to be a humanoid, in essence. You were supposed to be my… wife."

Luna breathes deeply for a moment, allowing the silence to wash over her as the truth of the matter weighs on her shoulders as a heavy boulder. "So… is that why…" She motions between them again.

"I think so - you see, when we were both retracted into the Upperworld again, our human essences couldn't be fully erased. So we're still programmed… for each other."

"Uh, okay. I guess that explains a lot."

Onyx nods. "It sure does. I'm just sorry I didn't explain it to you sooner."

"But there's one more thing I don't know."

"Ask away!"

Luna swallows for a moment before speaking. "Well, if you were the one destroyed, why is it that I wasn't allowed to live?"

Onyx frowns. "Well, the way I understand it, humanoids have little to no purpose without their significant life partner, so you were retracted because otherwise you would have been doomed to a life alone. Because I wouldn't have been there for you." His voice wavers a little as the verbalization of his worst fear takes shape in his mind.

Luna wraps her small arms around Onyx's strong torso. "I'm really glad I have you now."

"Me too, Luna. You are… so amazing. And for that, I am grateful."

CHAPTER 7

"Yeah I saw the little perp this morning… I had him in my sights, but he darted down an alleyway before I could catch him. No, Carnes, it wasn't the donuts slowing me down… you should've seen this kid, he was like *unnaturally* fast… yeah, yeah, I know, we gotta catch him. You're preaching to the choir here, Carnes. Okay, okay. Yeah I'll keep my eyes peeled. Last I saw him was at the intersection of Cranberry and Sasquatch. Yep, over and out."

Officer Jones ends his phone call, and continues making the long trek back to his office from the coffee shop.

I was so close… I almost had him. If only I was just a little faster. Maybe I really should be eating a little healthier.

He glances down at his distended, donut-filled belly, and shrugs. *It's a nice thought but I really doubt I could survive all this craziness without my coffee and donuts.*

Upon reaching his office, he settles down at his desk, and decides to look over the various police reports involving the suspicion around this mysterious, blue-clad figure. There have only been a few thus far, and only within the span of about a week, but it was better than nothing. A lead is a lead, no matter how sparse it may seem at first.

He picks up one of the security camera photos and takes a good, long look at Seth as a chill runs down his spine. He shivers, but remains focused.

"I *will* find you, and when I do, you'll curse the day you were born. No one upsets my town and gets away with it… *no one.*"

✳✳✳

As the scorned child moves toward the abode of the heroes, the sky seems to darken in his wake. What was once an azure sky dotted with immaculate, puffy white clouds, is now darkening to a sickly gray, with even the clouds seemingly trying to escape. A cool breeze follows him as he makes his way to the main entrance of the building. His small, bony hand grips the cold metal of the door handle, and he struggles to push it open.

It seems there is a force field keeping me from entering this area. He mutters a few newly learned expletives that he picked up from overhearing other Earth-dwellers, and then steps back to get a better look at the obstacle at hand. His eyes widen with insight as they quickly land on the word "PULL" printed obviously on the glass door. He smiles gleefully and does as the written text instructs him, thereby granting him access to the building. He continues walking toward the front desk, past a rather plump woman quietly reading a magazine in a nearby chair, and is immediately greeted with the superior gaze of the woman behind the desk.

"May I help you?" She lowers her glasses to get a better look at him - likely to compensate for the bifocal effect.

"Yes, I would greatly appreciate your assistance."

The woman scans his body with her eyes and points toward a doorway down the hallway behind her. "Comic con is going to be held down the hall, but you're a day early - it doesn't start until tomorrow."

Seth slowly turns his head at a slight angle, as if an invisible noose is holding him by the throat and had just broken his neck. "What is… comic con?"

The jaunty angle likely appears unnatural to the woman, as she begins to curiously stare him down again.

"You mean that is really just how you dress?"

Her rude query is met with silence. "Well, okay then. What did you need from me?"

Seth tilts his head slowly back to its original posture, and meets her eyes with his cold, dead, violet ones.

"I need to find Luna and Onyx."

"Do they have a last name?"

More silence.

"Are they residents here?"

A pause. "What is… 'resident'?"

The woman behind the desk stiffens, as she realizes the abnormality of the situation. "Who are you, and why are you here? I'm going to need to see some sort of identification, or I am going to have to ask you to leave."

"What is… 'identification'?"

"Uhm, okay. Just remain where you are. Hey, you're wearing the same weird outfit that other guy was wearing..." She not-so-subtly shifts her weight, landing her hip on the concealed panic button behind the counter.

"What are you doing?" For a newly Earth-bound being, Seth catches even the subtlest of motions.

"Nothing that concerns you. Now, I suggest you either leave, or wait quietly for - "

She never gets to finish that sentence, as Seth's fist comes into direct contact with her unsuspecting skull, and her mortal body folds onto the floor in a disorganized heap. A slow trickle of blood trickles out of her nose and her eyes remain closed amidst the sickly pallor of her complexion. He wastes no time in leaping over the counter and looking through the records to find information about Luna and Onyx's whereabouts. After only a few minutes of searching, he manages to find their names amongst the other listed residents, and he makes note of their house number.

Now I will be able to find them, and do what I came to Earth to do. Finally!

He tries (and fails) to hide the delirious glee that spreads across his face - the sheer proximity of his target makes his skin tingle in anticipation. His hand grips the hilt of the dagger concealed in his pocket, while the other hand checks to make sure the magnetized rock is at hand to transport him back to the Upperworld once the deed is done.

CHAPTER 8

“Okay, but is that really going to work? It sounds… crazy.” The red-haired sorter asks Evander expectantly, as the plan he suggested seems to be nothing short of bizarre. It’s raucous, discordant, and quite risky. Evander slowly nods his head - he clearly has weighed the options, and doesn't actually care at all.

“Yes Brielle, I’m convinced it’s our only option. You’re going to have to trust me on this one. Can you do that?”

She nods, but continues biting her lip nervously. “I really hope you’re right, Evander. It’s just, crazy.”

He turns to respond to her, but his jaw is set stiffly, and his face has been hardened from all the planning and organizing of this rogue mission. It would be a lot for anyone, but especially someone who is still just the record keeper. Evander was never meant to lead a revolution - but here he is, doing it anyway. Mostly because no one else would, and someone *has to,* or else their existence in the Upperworld really would end forever. The measures he is taking are all working against the impending apocalypse that is set to occur if Zephyr is allowed to decease without a replacement. And in this case, Onyx has been chosen to fulfill that role.

It will be okay, it will be okay. He mumbles this mantra to himself while inhaling the tepid air of the Upperworld deeply. It usually calms him, but it seems that the closer they get to the enacting of this plan, even the mantra has lost its power on him. Evander tries not to let that scare him though. No - he's got far more important things to think of, things that could either make him stronger, or completely crush him under the weight of their importance.

"Evander? Evander!" Brielle shakes him out of his silence.

"Yes?"

"I wanted to say… thank you."

"For what?"

"I mean, you're just… taking control over a scary situation. The only reason I'm not too worried about it is… that you've got it under control."

Evander forces a weak smile, but feels like it's filled with lies. "I don't -" He stops himself before saying something that might make her needlessly fearful. "Um, you are welcome. I'll do my best. In the meantime, the best thing you can do is to just stay calm."

She nods, and heads back toward her pod. Evander exhales loudly, hoping beyond high hope that he holds it together long enough not to let anyone down - that has always been his worst fear.

If it's the last thing I do, I will make sure Zephyr doesn't win. Even if I have almost no idea what I'm doing. After all, Onyx will be here soon, and when he gets here, he'll know what to do. At least, I hope he will, because I'm afraid I don't.

✱✱✱

"Ready to head out, Luna? There is much we have to do to facilitate our lives on Earth. These things take time, but they have to be done."

Luna shrugs her shoulders. "Like what, exactly? We already went shopping yesterday." She motions toward the bags of clothing that they bought.

"That is true, but there are other things we will need, like a personal vehicle, and a mobile cellular device for each of us."

"Huh?"

"You'll see, I'll explain it all as we go. Just stuff to allow us to fit in better. I've already spoken with my contact at the registry, who is going to supply us with social security numbers."

Luna continues to look at him with a blank stare. "I am not at all sure what you're talking about."

"That's okay, for now. But I'm really not leaving you here alone, so come on now." He motions his hand toward the door, and Luna begrudgingly follows, as she looks around at their new, comfortable home.

"We'll be back later, you know. Just a few errands to run first."

"But what about -"

"I'm not going to let him hurt you."

"But what if -"

"No 'what-ifs'. Nothing is going to happen to you, Luna. I swear on my life, okay?"

She nods, but the fear doesn't leave her eyes. Onyx frowns sadly, and gently squeezes her hand, feeling defeated by the sad reality that he could never fully eradicate the anxiety that she holds.

"Alright, come on now. Lots to do! First stop, cell phones!" Onyx plasters on a smile, since having a cell phone, especially as advanced as they are these days, would hopefully be a fun new experience. But Luna remains skeptical.

"Look, I can't help you unless you let me. So, let's go!"

She nods and moves through the open door he props with his arm. "Good."

"So there is a vendor that sells these cellular devices just a few blocks away. I already searched the approximate location through the computer that is located in our house."

Luna nods politely, but seems like she is a million miles away. Her violet eyes seem to rest on the nearby horizon line, and rarely meet Onyx's gaze. But he contents himself with guiding her to their location.

CHAPTER 9

The long, dark hair of the child cascades over his sullen expression. He locates the home where Onyx and Luna were documented to inhabit and peers through the windows, but he cannot find them anywhere.

Where are they? They were supposed to be here. Why aren't they here?

He scratches his smooth chin and continues to awkwardly pace around the perimeter of the property. He is about to give up and try to find them a different way when he catches a glint of long, dark, hair blowing in the breeze. He hesitates for a moment, since the figure with the long hair isn't wearing Luna's typical pink jumpsuit, but his notion is finally confirmed upon the recognition of the man she is with.

Finally... finally!

He lets out a hearty laugh that carries on the warm breeze, and too late, he notices that he has caught the attention of his targets. She turns and looks at him, squinting her eyes in the brief shard of sunlight breaking through the darkening cloud cover, until recognition shows on her face and she screams, hiding behind her companion. He pulls her close, and visually searches for the source of her fright, until his eyes land on Seth, who is rapidly approaching them. He grabs her hand and takes off running, but Seth is faster, and is about to catch up to them.

Almost there!

His hand finds the dagger in his pocket, and clenches it excitedly as his moment of revenge seems to finally approach.

The girl trips over a rock and falls onto the concrete. The man with her hurriedly tries to help her up, but her attacker steadily approaches. His hand closes around the dagger in his pocket, and he pulls it out, ready to stab it into her heart. A bit stunned, the girl gets up and starts running while being pulled along by her companion. But Seth is faster, and steadily decreases the distance between them.

I've almost got it, in just a few short minutes, I'll have ended Luna once and for all, and I can return to the Upperworld to be Zephyr's right-hand man.

As he rapidly approaches, he locks eyes with Onyx for a moment, just long enough for him to sense the fear that he incites. *Good.* He sneers with delight, as his hand is armed with his weapon of choice.

I'm going to plunge this into her heart, but I'll take him out too, if I have to. Seth follows them into a back alley, where they are trapped on three sides by two brick buildings and a chain link fence. *Perfect. Now they have nowhere to run.*

"Onyx! He's coming!" She shrieks, but it doesn't stop his measured, imminent approach.

"I can see that, Luna! Get behind me. NOW!" She willingly complies, as some nearly inaudible whimpers escape from her pale lips.

***

"What the hell happened here?"

Officer Carnes stands over the crime scene surrounding the unconscious woman at the front desk who was obviously attacked. The paramedics had also arrived, and are now loading her unconscious body into an ambulance on a stretcher. The sterile white of the sheets seem to frame her limp form like a burial shroud. The paramedics seem hopeful for a smooth recovery based on a quick check-over, but they are rushing her to the hospital for a more thorough evaluation.

"Well, there was obviously an assault, and it seems there may have been some injuries sustained. We're still investigating the suspect, but it's inconclusive at the moment."

Officer Carnes nods. "Yeah, I gathered that much. But what do you think *happened*? So some guy just came in here and attacked the receptionist? There's always a motive, but I can't find one yet. Was it a robbery?"

The detective shakes his head. "No, after speaking with the other employees, and comparing transaction records for the morning, it appears that monetarily, everything is accounted for."

Carnes scratches the back of his neck. "Well then, it means they were after *something else…*"

The detective nods. "I'd wager it was information they wanted. But what kind of valuable information is kept in a condo facility? It's not news that people live here. So what's the big secret?"

"Maybe they were looking for *someone* who lives here."

"Perhaps. It's inconclusive, as I've said."

Officer Carnes shifts his focus to the crowd of facility employees and emergency responders. "Do you know if there were any eye-witnesses at the scene of the crime?"

"Not sure yet, we're still in the questioning process. But, given the public nature of the scene, I wouldn't be surprised if someone saw what happened and could give us a description of the attacker."

"I saw the guy."

Both Officer Carnes and the detective turn around to see a rather heavy-set woman who seems a bit shaken from the ordeal that she witnessed.

"Ma'am, I certainly appreciate you stepping forward in this trying time. If you could describe what you saw, as precisely as possible, that would be greatly helpful to our case."

She quickly nods, her double chin nearly merging with her broad neck. "Well, I was sitting here just reading a copy of *Women's Monthly* while waiting for my boyfriend to finish clocking out. We had plans to get lunch, since we never get to spend time together, and -"

The detective politely raises his hand, as a signal for her to pause. "That's all good and fine, but the perpetrator… we need to know who did this to Mallory. Surely, she didn't affront him to require such treatment - she's worked here for a long time. I need you to take a deep breath, and try to think about what the guy looked like. Can you do that for me? I know you're scared, but I need you to try."

The rotund woman nods again, as her face turns a bit red with embarrassment and nerves. "Okay, so basically I was just sitting here, reading up on the latest waxing trends - you know, for bikini season…"

Officer Carnes exchanges a cringe with the detective, and then they both look back at their witness.

"… and then I see this peculiar character walk in the lobby. He had dark, black hair, was about, oh I don't know, maybe almost six feet tall, but not quite. Oh, and he was wearing this really bizarre, powder-blue jumpsuit."

The color instantly drains out of Officer Carnes' face as the synapses connect in his brain. His eyes widen for a moment, until he manages to compose himself. "Thank you so much for your help, ma'am. I think I know who did this."

"You do?" The woman and the detective say in unison.

"Yeah, your description matches a very shady character I've been trying to track down for over a week now. That little perp has been trespassing on private property, threatening locals with a knife, and just generally causing a lot of fear around town. The next chance I get, I am going to bring him in for questioning, with some possible legal action to follow."

The woman nods again. "Anything else I can do for you, Officer?"

"Well, now that I have an idea who did this, I suppose the next thing I should ask you is, exactly *what* did he do?"

"Well, I saw him speaking with Mallory at the desk, and she was understandably uncomfortable, as he seems very off-putting, especially for a lady - if you catch my drift. And so, I think she must have pushed a panic button or something, and he saw her do that so he clocked her right in the noggin. She was out like a light, and then he jumped clear over the desk and started thumbing through papers. I have no idea why - I noticed he didn't take anything, just looked around for a couple minutes."

"Thank you ma'am, you have been most helpful. You are free to go."

She nods again, and then makes her way out the front door, presumably to meet up with her boyfriend.

"Well, detective, I really do think I have a lead on this one."

"Great! And do you know where the perp went?"

"That's the only thing I'm still sniffing out, as of late. But I'll find him, and when I do, he'll regret the day he was born."

CHAPTER 10

Onyx's breathing intensifies, and he feels his whole body shake as Seth approaches. He sees the sneer forming on his face, as Seth's lips curve into a few harsh lines and his deep purple eyes are piercing. But that is nothing compared to the dagger firmly gripped in his wiry fingers.

Luna's small body shakes violently, as she presses herself firmly behind Onyx's strong, but uncertain frame. She grabs his hand for a brief moment, and gives it a quick squeeze. Luna trembles as she hides behind Onyx, uncertain of what madness Seth might unleash on them next.

Never taking his eyes off of Onyx's, Seth places his hand on Onyx's shoulder, which Onyx then throws off quickly to recoil and blocks Seth's punch. Onyx takes the next moment to sidekick Seth, causing him to collapse to the ground as his knees buckle. Landing on top of him, Onyx begins to pummel his pale face. The violet eyes stare back at him, numb and emotionless. Onyx only gets a few punches in before Seth manages to twist his ankle around Onyx's and flip him over, gaining the upper hand for the moment. Onyx stares up at him as the dagger finds its place at his jugular.

"NO! Stop! Onyx!" Luna squeals in utter despondency as her vulnerability fills the air. She crumbles to the ground as the two men continue to fight to the death. Onyx, noticing her despair, boils over with rage. He lays into Seth furiously, shoving his head into the ground with a terrible crack. Seth pushes Onyx away and stands, shaky, then moves toward her.

He wastes no time in placing the dagger at Luna's neck, and a small whimper escapes from her pink lips as his bony arms trap her in his grasp. Seth hesitates to plunge it into her major artery. He stares at her for a second before he's back on the ground. Onyx now stands over Seth with a blood stained brick in his hand. Seth lies on the ground moaning, not quite out, but nonetheless dazed.

Seth trips Onyx, causing him to fall on top of him. Onyx grabs Seth by the shoulders, picks him up, and throws him against the brick wall behind them. The sneer returns, and the knife that was once at Luna's neck is at Onyx's. He winces as slight pressure on the blade produces stinging pain, and a small trickle of blood runs down his neck.

Grabbing the offending wrist, Onyx tries to overpower him, but Seth's lithe and wiry figure easily wiggles out of his grasp - he clearly has more finesse in combat than Onyx has. After escaping his grasp, Seth tackles Onyx to the ground, as the small cut on his neck continues to bleed. His smaller frame lands on top of Onyx, and the dagger resumes its position as the attacker's lips part just long enough to verbalize the threat hanging in the air.

"Let me kill her, and I'll leave you alone."

"Never!"

Onyx recoils at the affront to Luna, and channels that rage into flipping Seth onto his back. He reaches for the dagger, but it remains tightly in Seth's grasp.

Luna quietly slips past the fight and runs away to find safety in the nearby park, sobbing as she runs.

"Give me the dagger, and I'll make sure you don't suffer. I'll make it quick and painless, which is much more than you deserve!"

Bracing himself against the ground, Onyx manages to keep Seth from moving, but the dagger seems locked in the impenetrable coil of Seth's grimy fingers. His sour breath assaults Onyx's face, but he stays focused, until he notices that Luna is nowhere to be found.

"Luna? Where is *she*?" He pauses just long enough for Onyx to grab the blade from his hand, and he uses his broad shoulders to trap him against the brick wall again.

"Nowhere you will ever find her, I'm sure. Now give me one reason why you *shouldn't* suffer intensely for what you've done."

"What *I've* done? *You* are the one who kept the secrets from her. You kept her in the dark for far too long. Am I *really* the one at fault here? Or is it *you*?"

Seth grins malevolently from his manipulative attempt at throwing Onyx off his game, but Onyx remains stoic. Onyx's hands tremble with fear as he begins to lower Seth's dagger slowly to his pale neck.

"You deserve the worst torture imaginable, but since I don't have that readily available, I'll just let you bleed out." Onyx readies himself to apply enough pressure to the dagger to break his skin, but suddenly, Seth's eyes glaze over and begin to shine, like some other violet eyes he knows far too well.

Luna...

Sirens can be heard wailing in the distance. Onyx hesitates to make the kill, and Seth smiles. "The authorities are coming. If you take too much longer to kill me, they're going to arrest you and ask questions later. Make your choice, Onyx Dalton Miller."

He shudders at the sound of his Earth name - the name he was supposed to have had if his mother had not aborted him four centuries ago. But it also makes him angry, and it's enough anger for him to push the knife directly into Seth's neck. A pathetic moan escapes from his lips, but he is still alive.

"Enjoy the Underworld, Seth. It's where you belong, after all." And with that, Onyx runs away from the scene, leaving the dagger in Seth's outstretched, weakening hand as his life energy slowly fades from his lean body.

Onyx runs toward the park where he assumes Luna must be, but he turns to look back at Seth for a split second, and he realizes the magnitude of his actions. Killing is new to him, and it's not pleasant, even if Seth had threatened Luna and tracked her unceasingly. It will be easier to sleep with the knowledge that he is out of the picture, but taking a life is sickening, and there is now blood on his hands that he will have to live with for the rest of his mortal life on Earth.

CHAPTER 11

Brielle goes back to the Sorting Room after the meeting with Evander to work her shift. The work takes her mind off of everything, which is good, because the stress and fear she feels about her potentially impending doom is definitely beginning to take its toll on her. Evander did his best to reassure her that everything is under control, but somehow, she still questions how much stock she can put in his confidence. She wants to believe it, but somehow, she just can't.

She is jolted out of her silent thoughts by someone rudely bumping into her shoulder, almost making her drop the orb she is carrying.

"Hey! You gotta be careful here, I almost dropped this!" She turns to face the person who hip-checked her, and she is met with Jade's stoic eyes.

"Whatever, it's all going to Hell anyway." She rolls her eyes and saunters away with her silver hair trailing behind her.

She has got to get a grip - she's just mad because Onyx was chosen to be Zephyr's replacement, and not her. Anyways, gotta focus. Don't mess this up.

Brielle has been extra careful about making sure everything is done accurately, what with the fiasco surrounding the Luna and Delphine mess. It is too important of a job to ever take lightly, but after the mix-up happened, she's policed herself even more.

And... perfect. She eases the orb into the appropriate glowing receptacle, and then goes back to the tagging station, per usual. She glances at one of the digitized clocks on the wall, and then looks back at her schedule.

Just a few more Earth minutes to go until I'm done. Stay focused. She hums softly to herself and then reaches for the next orb. She places it perfectly, and smiles to herself as the screen above it lights up with the images of new life. But to her left, she notices a sorter panicking as their screen lights up, but remains blank. There are no sirens, or red flashing lights, so it can't be a mistake, but something is certainly going on.

"Hey, everything okay over here?" Brielle looks over to the younger sorter next to her.

"Yes, I do believe so. But, the screen doesn't look like yours…" He points to the screen in front of Brielle which currently is broadcasting images of a small child with a backpack going to school.

"Indeed, that is strange. Let me see what's going on, maybe someone can help." Brielle looks around for any sign of an emergency, and seeing none, she relaxes a bit, but cannot shake the feeling that something is more than a little *off.* She continues walking around the Sorting Room, hoping to find answers in the large crowd of sorters going about their daily work.

Upon a closer look around, Brielle notices a few more screens that have lit up in just a plain, ghastly white.

But that's the only thing - still no sirens, and still no foggy tubes.

I*t can't possibly be a mix-up like before, this isn't the same... or, is it?*

She scratches the back of her neck as she waits for further instructions. The other sorters are beginning to notice the anomaly, and are beginning to become upset. But there are still no answers to be had. Brielle continues to nervously pace around the large room, in the hopes that the problem will be explained shortly. After a few moments of this uncertainty, she recognizes the back of Evander's head, and taps him on the shoulder.

"Oh, Evander - I was wondering if you had any idea... about what may be causing the white screens? It is not normal, after all, and it is quite... concerning."

"Yes, we are still exploring the issue. I honestly have no idea what might be causing it. It's definitely not a mishap like... before. So don't worry about that." He pauses for a moment to click a few buttons at a nearby receptacle where the screen is blank white.

"From what I can see at the moment, nothing is responsive, which means that although the orbs were sorted correctly as Zephyr had intended, they have likely failed to connect to their respective life forces and Earthly forms."

"What does that mean?" Brielle's face starts to pale as Evander continues to fiddle with the buttons on one screen, and then another, but to no avail.

"Well, I've never really seen this before, but it looks like there's a malfunction at the head?"

"The head?"

Evander pulls Brielle to the side, away from the earshot of other sorters. "Please do not panic, because if you do, the others will panic, and then there will be nothing but chaos."

"Evander, what is going on?"

He takes a deep breath, and then continues. "It seems, that the end is near. Zephyr is dying."

"I knew that. But what's happening now?"

"No, you don't understand. Zephyr *is* the connector between the ethereal realm of the Upperworld, and Earth. The connection is failing, because he is dying… right *now*."

"Oh my pod, what do we… what do we do?"

Evander clamps a firm but gentle hand over Brielle's trembling mouth. "Remain calm, Brielle. You'll only frighten the others."

"But I'm frightened!"

"Shhhh! This is go-time. We are going to call an emergency meeting, and begin the change-over process."

"But, what about Jade?"

"What about her?"

"She's mad… really mad, about what happened."

"It doesn't matter what she thinks. There are bigger things at stake. We need to remember that the future of the Upperworld is in our hands, and there isn't a moment to lose! Go now, rally the troops. The time has come."

CHAPTER 12

"Yeah Jones, there is no doubt in my mind that it was the same kid who attacked the condo receptionist. I'm aware that it's a little vague, but honestly, how many people actually fit that description? I think it's pretty obvious. Besides, he's been creating enough unrest around town, I'm really not surprised that he's responsible for this too. It's high time that he be brought to justice… No I do not think 'Wanted' posters would be appropriate in this situation. And I also do not appreciate your hilarious gag reel, Jones. Smarten up! This kid needs to be caught, I am so serious… Okay, yep… Yeah, I agree… Glad we're on the same page. I'm just gonna take a drive-around town, and see if I can find anything suspicious happening. I'll keep you posted. Yeah yeah, over-and-out."

Officer Carnes continues driving around town as he planned, in hopes that the perpetrator would be visible from the vantage point of his car. He turns his attention to the radio momentarily, as he settles into one of his favorite talk shows on the sports channel. He's fully enthralled by some of the latest baseball stats when he sees what looks like a body on the ground, covered in blood, and surrounded by police cars. He immediately pulls over to it, and grabs his two-way radio.

He quickly exits his vehicle, and recognizes the guy on the ground.

"What's going on here?" *It's him… but how? What happened?*

"Male, looks to be about age eighteen or so, deceased from a stab wound, from what we can see so far. We'll know more after the coroner's report."

"Okay but you don't understand... I know this kid!"

"You *know* him?"

"Yes, well, not like that. I mean, I've been trying to track him down for weeks."

"Oh, is - was he the perp you were going on and on about?"

Officer Carnes rolls his eyes, and then nervously shuffles his feet. He's never been good with death, even when it's someone problematic. One thing he always tries not to let on to anyone, is that underneath that hard and crusty exterior, is a big teddy bear of a guy who really does hate to see anyone suffer.

"Yeah, he most certainly was."

"Well, no need to worry about him anymore."

"Guess not. Coroner's on the way, you said?"

"Yep, it's all set. But I'm going to need to figure out how this happened. Whoever did this, is an even greater threat to our town than this guy was."

"That's true, did you check for fingerprints on the weapon?"

"No, not yet."

"All right, I'm on it."

Officer Carnes walks back to his police car to grab some sterile white gloves and other tools out of the trunk. He returns to the scene of the crime, and gingerly grabs the bloody knife from the fatal wound it is still stuck in. The knife is covered in congealed blood, the once bright-red blood cells turning a dried up, sticky, rusty brown. After analyzing the hilt of the dagger, Officer Carnes sighs and walks back to where the other officers are milling around.

"There are prints, but they don't match any of the criminals in the system. So it seems there's a new one in town."

The other officer nods. "Indeed. Okay, we gotta ID the murderer, STAT. If someone is posing a threat to the good people of this town, I won't stand for it."

***

"Luna? Is that you?"

Anthony sees her from across the street as she's running away from the fight.

"Anthony? Anthony!" Luna wastes no time running across the street, momentarily forgetting to use the crosswalk. Her erratic jaywalking elicits some frustrated honking from the nearby cars who swerve to avoid hitting her.

"Luna, you've got to be careful! What were you thinking running into the street like that?"

She buries her head in his shoulder, and he reciprocates with a friendly hug, much to Miranda's dismay.

"Yeah, so she stupidly ran in front of some cars. We've all done it, what's the big deal?"

Anthony makes eye contact with Miranda and rolls his eyes. He lowers his voice a bit.

"She's clearly upset, chill out. I don't know what happened but she's terrified and needs help. I'll just be a sec."

Miranda crosses her arms but ends up begrudgingly walking toward the fountain to sun herself on the edge of it while snapping selfies for her social media pages.

"Luna, are you okay? You've gotta tell me what happened. And where's Onyx?"

Her lower lip trembles as the words tumble out of her mouth. "He was protecting me."

"From what?"

"Someone who wanted to hurt me."

"Oh my gosh…"

"And so I ran away because I was scared…"

"… and you found me." Anthony pauses to absorb the information that she is slowly disclosing.

"Yes. And now I don't know what to do…"

"He'll come for you, I'm sure. Did he know which direction you ran."

She nods. "Yes, I think he saw me run."

"Okay, okay well that's good! I mean, I'm sure he'll be right here before you know it." Anthony gently pats her on the shoulder, and then begins to walk toward Miranda. "I should, probably get back to her. She'll be mad if I keep her waiting too long and -"

"No, stay."

"Huh?"

"I mean, can you help me? I really don't know where he is, and I'm very frightened."

Anthony sighs. "Okay, I'll stay with you until he gets here. I mean, couldn't you just call him though?"

"*Call* him?"

"Yeah, with your cellphone?"

Her face doesn't register the term or the concept.

"Oh, you have no idea what that is, do you? Okay. Yeah, I'll wait right here with you. Or, better yet, why don't we both go sit with Miranda?"

Luna hesitates, but eventually nods, and they both walk over to where Miranda is seated on the edge of the fountain.

"Oh, hey *Luna*." She draws out her name as if it is a great inconvenience for her to say it out loud.

"Hello, Miranda."

"I see you've changed out of that ridiculous pink rubbery number."

"Huh?"

Anthony glares at Miranda. "Come on, just be cool, okay? I really don't think that was necessary. She's not… from around here and just needed some time to adjust. Isn't that right, Luna?"

Luna nods, but she can't help but notice the strange dynamic that is developing between the three of them. She contents herself with looking up at the bright-blue early afternoon sky after the clouds broke apart, and she tries to breathe deeply and relax until Onyx can get back to her.

He'll be here, I just know it. Any second now.

CHAPTER 13

Brielle nods quickly, and then runs off to tell everyone what she heard from Evander, all while trying not to panic.

This is really happening. We're going to take down Zephyr today. It all comes down to this.

She tries to regulate her breathing, but she knows that she is on the cusp of a panic attack, and that if she doesn't calm down, it's going to be a full-blown episode. Being a sorter in the Upperworld is already stressful enough without the added pressure of overthrowing the supreme and powerful leader. But that is exactly what she is doing, and Brielle is doing the best she can to be okay with that.

Find the others... maybe Griffin. She runs to the wall with the digital schedule on it, and searches for Griffin's name and location. *He's in the record keeping office, of course!*

She wastes no time in running to the record keeping office. When she gets there, she knocks on the door to get his attention. She can't open it herself because she isn't a record keeper, and her handprint wouldn't be recognized by the scanner.

"Oh, hello Brielle. Is there something I can do for you?"

"Zephyr is dying now and it's time to put the plan into action. Spread the word, and get ready." The words tumble out of her mouth at a rapid rate.

"What? How do you know?"

"The screens in the Sorting Room… are blank."

"Like before? Was there another mix-up?"

Brielle sighs as she searches for the right terms to convert the message properly. Behind Griffin, the record keeping office is colored by the various blinks and beeps of the various computers and gadgets that are housed there.

"No, there wasn't a mix-up, but the orbs aren't… connecting, that's what Evander said. They aren't connecting to their human forms, something like that. Whatever it is, it's bad. Prepare yourself for the switch over!"

"Okay, so where's Onyx?"

Brielle's eyes widen. "You mean, he hasn't been transported back here yet?"

"Not to my knowledge, no…"

"I hope Evander's on top of that…"

She waits for a further response from Griffin, and finding none, she turns on her heel to find Evander.

He's gotta get Onyx back here!

Her feet move as fast as they can back toward the Sorting Room, but she also doesn't want to make the others nervous or stir up a mass panic. If that happens, then they'll definitely all be doomed. After what feels like the longest walk of her existence, Brielle enters the Sorting Room again, and even more screens are pale white. In fact, she'd be hard-pressed to find one that isn't. After a brief run-through of the main area, she finds Evander feverishly telling other Disturbers what is going on and doling out personalized instructions.

"Evander!"

Brielle interrupts his conversation, and he looks none too pleased, but allows her to speak anyway.

"Brielle, now is really not the time for -"

"Onyx. Is he here yet?"

Evander's face turns as white as the screens in the Sorting Room. "I… I can't believe the most important part of the plan slipped my mind!" He jogs out of the Sorting Room with Brielle following him toward the transport room. "I have to program the machine to bring him back, and it's going to take a little time, which we don't exactly have. Please notify everyone of this latest development, and let them know that they may need to fight. Start to form a coalition in the Grand Hall, and I'll arrive with Onyx shortly."

Brielle hesitates to move, as she is frozen in fear.

"GO!"

She is snapped out of her hesitation by his desperate plea, and runs back out of the transport room to find those involved with the coalition.

It's going to be okay, I can do this. I can do this. I really, really hope I can do this.

✳✳✳

"What do you mean the subject is untraceable? You mean to tell me, that there is *nothing* in the census to identify him? Yes, I really am shocked. This is… certainly unprecedented. Yes, okay. I'll keep asking around, of course. Okay, thank you for your time."

Officer Carnes ends the call with the coroner's office, and scratches his chin pensively. The coffee cup sitting on the table in front of him suddenly holds his interest as his thoughts get too loud for his own taste. Inhaling the warmth and the steam from the beverage, he breathes deeply, trying to avoid becoming too caught up in the craziness that is police work.

It will sort itself out eventually - it has too, logically. No one can defy logic.

His silent mantra comforts him a bit, but only for a moment, as he is interrupted by his phone ringing again.

"Hello? Yes, this is he. What? No, that's impossible… do you mean to tell me that the prints on the dagger don't match those of the subject? So it wasn't suicide? Okay, okay. I'll notify the other officers. Yes, we're on the case. Don't worry… I'll get the detective right on this. Okay. Will do, thanks."

He exhales as he ends yet another call, and while staring out the window, he quickly realizes the stark reality that this case may not be like anything he has ever seen before. Police work is never dull, and it can even be pretty thrilling. But it very rarely is this bizarre. Usually, everything can be explained with a very clear cause-and-effect relationship. But this is the exception - and anything beyond the realm of logic eludes him, and rightfully so. Logic is all he knows.

CHAPTER 14

"Luna! LUNA!"

She looks up from her polite conversation with Miranda and Anthony in the park to see Onyx running toward her, nearly out of breath. There is congealed blood splattered on his shirt, eliciting expressions of shock and confusion on the faces of the others.

"Onyx!" She runs toward him, leaving Miranda and Anthony a few paces behind her, and they embrace, even in the midst of the confusion and fighting that they both witnessed.

"I'm so glad I found you, when you ran off, I didn't know where you went."

Luna nods, but can't seem to take her eyes off of his bloody shirt. "I know, but, what's all this?"

Onyx's face turns white. "Well, humans have bodily fluids that tend to… leak sometimes." Luna nods, and then her eyes move to the cut on his neck.

"Is that what happened to your neck?"

Onyx nods slowly. "But… we're safe now." He fights the smile that is turning up at the corners of his lips, but that smile is simultaneously filled with pain.

Luna's face subconsciously mirrors his, and she raises an eyebrow. "Do you mean…"

"*He* won't be bothering us anymore."

"For real?"

"Completely real."

She wraps her arms around him in another hug, and smiles. But she notices Onyx's pensive, blank stare and she presses her lips tightly together.

"Then why aren't you happy now?"

Onyx sighs, and runs his hand through his pale blonde hair. Then he gently pulls Luna closer, as to keep their conversation out of the others' earshot. Lowering his voice, he does his best to explain morality to Luna in a way that she can understand.

"Well, you don't quite understand, Luna. I had to take his life, to protect you."

"Okay?" Luna has trouble finding the gravity of the situation. "He was a bad person, it had to happen."

"Yes and no. Many people would agree with you, and part of me does. But I'm still torn about it because it wasn't necessarily Zephyr's outcome, and deviating from that often produces disaster, as you've seen. Who am I to decide when a person lives or dies? That is one of the many reasons that killing is wrong."

Luna blinks a few times, and then slowly nods. "I understand."

"Well, it's a very complex moral issue, so I understand if you don't. But we have to figure out a way to keep on living, even in the wake of this happening. We can still have a very happy life together, you and I. I hope you know that."

"I do, but I still think you should be happy - this is a good thing. It's *good* that he's gone." Onyx nods but remains pensive.

"In some ways, yes, but in some ways, no. I wasn't intending to kill him, I really didn't want to, but he gave me no choice - it was self-defense and -"

Luna cuts him off once again by placing her lips on his and kissing him passionately, right there in the park in front of Miranda and Anthony. Onyx heartily reciprocates, and murmurings of Anthony in the background are heard by both of them.

"See, Miranda? I told you nothing was going on. She's with Onyx."

Miranda nods but keeps her arms crossed. "I hear ya, Anthony. I really do. And I'm starting to believe you, but it's taking time."

He nods, and plants an innocent kiss on her lips. "I understand - it's okay. But I want you to know that I really, really love you."

She smiles at him - those three words always break down the walls she puts up. "I love you too, Anthony. More than I thought I'd ever love anyone, actually. And that's what scares me."

He puts his arm around her and pulls her close. "That's okay, we can be scared together."

In this moment, both couples are in blissful existence with one another, but sirens start to wail in the distance. Onyx begins to grow worried.

"Luna, my clothes… this is going to look bad - but we *have to* get home so I can clean this off."

Confusion shows on her face, but she nods. "I think I got some on myself too."

"Yes, but there's more on me. Come on, we need to move *now*."

Luna readily agrees and runs after Onyx as they both leave the park. She opens her mouth to ask him another question, but she is harshly interrupted.

"KEEP YOUR HANDS UP! NOW! GET ON THE GROUND!"

A police officer's gun is pointed at them, and Luna begins to softly cry.

"Luna, just do what he says, there's nothing else we can do." Onyx's words register in her mind, and she does as he says. But as he slowly lowers himself down to the cold, hard concrete, his body slowly vaporizes into thin air.

CHAPTER 15

"Onyx? Welcome back, my friend. There is much to do, so please listen closely."

Onyx opens his eyes, and slowly adjusts to the harsh light of the transport room.

"What? Evander… How did… what? I was just… WHERE IS LUNA?"

Evander slowly eases him off the table and clears his throat. "Onyx, I know you probably have a million questions, but I really don't have any time to explain. Zephyr is dying -"

"Yeah, obviously. We knew that already -"

"No. He is dying *now*. We have to get you to the Great Hall before the Underworld portal opens up -"

"No! I am not doing *anything* until you bring Luna here, do you understand? You had no right to bring me back here without my consent, or her knowledge. We were being questioned by the police and now she's probably scared out of her mind! Bring her here now or so help me I'll let every soul in this realm be sucked down into the depths of doom for eternity!"

Evander feverishly wipes a bead of sweat off of his forehead as Brielle nervously looks at the crowds of sorters beginning to panic outside the window of the transport room. "Um, we gotta hurry, Evander. It's getting pretty bad out there. It's only a matter of time…" She cannot bring herself to finish that sentence, as the implications surrounding it are far too painful to verbally acknowledge.

Evander sighs but eventually caves in to Onyx's pleas for Luna to be considered in the midst of this whole mess.

"You are absolutely right. Okay, Onyx, you've got to understand, we need you to replace Zephyr before he dies. We have a coalition lined up, ready to make the switch, but you've got to cooperate, and understand what you're getting into."

"Evander, he needs to suit up. Those Earth clothes won't be compatible with the life force energy he needs to connect with."

"You're absolutely right. I'll grab a spare one out of the closet here."

"Hey!" Onyx's voice cuts through their panic. "I am not doing *anything* until you get Luna here too."

Evander exchanges a feverish look with Brielle, who quickly nods. "We better do as he asks, we need him."

"Need me for what? What makes you think I can do this? You guys are acting quite irrationally. I'm not cut out for this!"

"Actually, you are. After extensive discussions, majority has ruled that you are the most apt for the job, since you are the only one with extensive immersive experiences living on both Earth and in the Upperworld. Also, you've studied just about everything there is to know about the human experience, which makes you perfectly qualified for the job. And you are our only hope to avoid doom.

Onyx slowly nods, and swallows his fear. "I understand, I won't let you down. But you have to bring Luna back before I agree to do anything."

Evander sighs, and rolls his eyes, but eventually relents. "I understand. Reanimate her here, Brielle. Onyx, put this on and dispose of those Earth clothes as quickly as possible." He hands him another pale blue jumpsuit, which is high-tech and will tailor itself once he puts it on to fit the precise dimensions of his body.

Onyx quickly disrobes while Brielle turns away to preserve his modesty, busying herself with finding Luna's exact coordinates on Earth to bring her back to the Upperworld. Evander leaves the transport room to check on the progress of the Disturbers.

"Can you find her?" Onyx asks desperately as he pulls the stretchy pants over his knees.

"I'm trying to, but it was harder than finding you. As a Head Guide, we have your DNA imprinted in the master system, which makes you a lot easier to locate. Sorters aren't in the system the same way, so it takes longer. Wait a second… oh okay. YES! I got her. Now let me just put a command into the machine and…"

She smiles nervously as the machine hums to life.

***

"Hey Carnes, where'd that guy go? He just disappeared into thin air!"

Luna shifts her gaze to her right, where Onyx was just a minute ago. "Onyx!"

"Quiet, ma'am. I'm gonna ask you to stay calm until we can figure out what's going on." The officer turns to his partner and looks at him incredulously. "Well he couldn't have disintegrated into thin air, so there's gotta be some explanation. Maybe he's an escape artist, like one of those Vegas magicians!"

"Johnson, this isn't the time for your joking, we have a suspect to track down -"

"I'm not joking! He was here, and then he was not…"

"This is serious, Johnson! Now get your head in the game! We gotta notify the station monitors and let them know what's going on…"

Their banter continues for a few minutes, but it feels like a hundred years to the terrified Luna, who has noticed Onyx's unexplained absence and now really has no idea where he could be. Her labored whimpers escape from her lips as she begins to cry. *Onyx where are you? Why did you leave me? You said you'd never leave me... what happened?* She fights the urge to become deliriously upset, as the police officers seem easily excitable in the wake of confusion. Her whole body shakes, and then she inhales before ascending into the next realm under the cover of darkness.

"Oh geez now the girl disappeared!"

"What are these people, a bunch of circus freaks?"

"What the-"

"Scan the perimeter! They can't have gone far!"

The group of officers begins to spread out, searching the vicinity for any sign of the mysterious girl and her lover with the blood on his hands. They run through the nearby streets, the alleyways, and even the usually tranquil park nearby with the calming water fountain. But they are nowhere to be found.

CHAPTER 16

"Hey Luna…"

Luna opens her brilliant violet eyes as she readjusts to the Upperworld.

"Onyx, where did you go? You left me there with those angry people with the guns and -"

"I know, I'm sorry, I didn't mean to, but I was needed here so Evander had me brought back."

"Why did they need you here? What's going on? I thought we weren't ever coming back! What happened?"

Onyx swallows quickly, and then tries to explain. "It seems that I'm needed as a replacement."

"A replacement for… what?"

"Well, Zephyr is…"

"He's dying, Luna, and we need Onyx to step up. If he doesn't, we all will spend eternity in the Underworld." Brielle jumps in to explain, and Onyx just slowly nods. He didn't want to shock Luna into cooperation, but given the gravity of the situation, he understands the need to hurry things along and worry about pleasantries later.

"Oh my pod, what are we going to do? Onyx, I'm scared, what do we do?" Onyx slides his arm around her on the table of the transport room.

"Well, we're going to do exactly what Evander tells us to do. He's the boss of this operation. Oh, and Jade will know what to do too -"

"Uh-uh." Brielle interrupts him nonchalantly, and shakes her head. "I guess we forgot to tell you… Jade has had some… strong feelings about the coalition, and has drifted from the greater good. So we're not collaborating with her anymore."

"Really? That is… shocking."

Luna nods her head. "That's scary. Any of us could turn at any moment…"

Onyx slowly nods, and gives her shoulder a slight squeeze. "Well, I think it's safe to say that at this point, anyone who is in is in, and anyone who is out, is out. Wouldn't you say so, Brielle?"

She nods, and then hands Luna an Upperworld suit. "Luna, you also need to shed those earth clothes as quickly as possible. You don't want to attract attention, plus you need to be able to move quickly. You only have a few moments before the revolution begins." With that, Brielle leaves the transport to join the others.

Luna doesn't hesitate to do as Brielle instructs her, and Onyx turns away out of respect, even though the two of them have very little to hide from each other at this point.

"Okay Luna, we need to run and meet up with everyone else. Are you ready?"

Luna nods, but then buries herself in Onyx's muscular chest. "I'm scared though."

"After all we've been through, haven't you learned? You've just got to do it afraid. I'm going to be the next ruler of humanity, and if you don't think I'm positively terrified, you'd be sorely mistaken."

"Okay, Onyx. I will do it afraid. But I wish I didn't have to."

Onyx pulls her close before they both hurriedly exit the transport room to meet up with the rest of the Disturbers. "Me too, Luna. Me too."

As they leave the transport room and embark on the biggest takedown in the history of humanity, the tepid air of the Upperworld seems to grow colder, and now all the life-bearing screens above the receptor tubes in the Sorting Room have been relegated to a deathly white.

"Are all these sorters part of the revolution?" Luna asks curiously, as the crowd seems to wind clear through the main doors of the Sorting Room and beyond.

"I'm not sure, but it seems like that is the case."

"Where's Evander?"

"I'm sure he is around here somewhere… Brielle and Griffin should be too."

They both quickly and effortlessly fall into step with the others, all the while hoping beyond high hope that the plans they have to take over will go smoothly and without any casualties. But of course, nothing goes perfectly, especially when the stakes are this high.

"Onyx! There you are. Come this way, we're going to bring you to the front so we can make the changeover as seamless as possible." Evander catches up to Onyx and Luna and carefully tugs his arm away from Luna. Her face becomes pained at being separated from him, and she is scared. At the last moment, his lips brush hers for a quick moment, much to Evander's disdain. Letting his breath mingle with hers, he mouths “do it afraid” and then follows Evander to the front of the crowd.

Luna stays where she is, allowing the people around her to get ahead of her, all while watching Onyx get pulled deep into the system, about to link himself to it forever. She swallows down the questions climbing up her throat, trying to remind herself that even though he showed her what love was - the honest, desperate need that was hidden below the surface that even she didn’t know existed until it was awakened - he was about to do something much more important. Never once did she think he would be the one to take over the reigns of everything. And now, too late, she begins to consider all that she herself must give up. That happy life that Onyx promised they would have on Earth definitely won’t be happening now. And as much as she hated Earth from the moment she first materialized on that fateful park bench, the place had become oddly familiar and comfortable to her, and it would not be an easy thing to give it up. As of late, she had even thought of having her own family with Onyx, but that definitely won’t happen now. As the crowds of people flow past her, Luna begins to mourn the loss of what could have been, all sacrificed for the greater good. She tells herself, and she knows, that deep down, it will be worth it. But even that seems ultimately inconsequential to what will soon be lost.

CHAPTER 17

"Look at them all running, and running toward what?" Jade says to no one in particular, cackling with glee as she looks over the crowd of sorters and guides marching swiftly toward the Grand Hall from her pod. She cackles decidedly as she taps her fingertips rhythmically on her side table.

"As if Onyx can save them. Why would he be able to?" She readies herself to do what she knows she was always meant to do, and opens the door, tugging her hood over her head to keep a low enough profile and get to the Throne Room before the coalition does. *They will thank me later for saving them from their own disastrous fate. And then, and only then, they will bow at my feet as the life force flows through my veins.*

She matches the footfalls of those around her, and gets all the way to the entrance of the Grand Hall before a tendril of her characteristic silver hair slips out of her hood and catches the eyes of a nearby sorter.

"Jade! What are you doing here?" His pointed finger assaults Jade's pride, and leaves her feeling embarrassed for a moment before her typical sneer returns.

"What am I doing? I'm doing what I should have done a long time ago - I am saving you from yourselves."

The sorter who called her out recoils, but the discomfort remains on his face. He visually searches around in his vicinity, but everyone seems to be in a trance.

"Everyone! Jade is here!" A few look over, their attention piqued at this point, but Jade is faster than they are, and she deftly squeezes through the sorters and guides in front of her while tucking her hair into her hood again. Blending into the crowd, she becomes one with those who disagree with her. It's a disturbing feeling of complicity, but she bites her lip and powers through the shame to move closer and closer to the front of the crowd. As she approaches, she can see Onyx, her competition, being guided by Evander toward the throne.

Look at them, so convinced their little idiotic plan is going to work. They are not powerful, but I am. I can save them. But they have to let me save them, and they will not. So I must get there before they can stop me.

As the crowd begins to converge at the entrance to the Grand Hall, a segment of the disturbers were predetermined to remove Zephyr's limp body from the throne, while others appear, ready to fight off the ones who are against the coalition, like the orderlies and sorters who falsely believe in Zephyr's rejuvenation and ultimate authority. She watches as they bring Onyx closer and closer to the throne amidst the bedlam unfolding in the crowd around them. The coalition seems to be fending off the dissenters quite effectively with their electrified spears and plasma cannons taken from the artillery department deep in the bowels of the Upperworld. She watches in utter glee as the violence continues to rage on, and the way that everyone seems to have their attention elsewhere. They're immortal in the Upperworld, but they can still inflict pain onto each other, which they are currently doing quite liberally.

This is far too easy. Is this really all it takes? Now I just have to get to the throne as soon as Zephyr is moved off of it.

She brazenly moves closer to it, but a loud rumble emanates from far below the ground, and she knows she is not imagining it, as the others seem to notice it too.

"What is that?" Evander turns toward Onyx at the front of the crowd, and his face turns white.

"It cannot be anything good. And something tells me we have to hurry - time is running out!"

Onyx is quite correct in his assessment of the situation, since the moment those words leave his mouth, a great, fiery, cavernous hole opens directly in front of the throne, and begins to steadily grow in diameter.

"What the -" Evander inserts a choice expletive that he probably picked up during his time doing Earth studies to be the record keeper.

Looking deep into the chasm, it becomes quite clear what it is, as the fiery insides begin to pick up momentum and creates a strong gust of wind - which never usually happens in the Upperworld.

Onyx swallows hard. "That's the entrance to the Underworld, and it will consume us all if we don't hurry." Then he turns to the now-panicking crowd. "Everyone, stay back! And stay calm!"

Evander grips his arm tighter. "Let's get you on that throne, and close this thing up." Onyx nods, and they both run around the perimeter of the circular chasm, leaving enough space between it and them so that they won't fall in. The air directly adjacent to it begins to warm up rapidly, but it isn't the tepid serenity of the Upperworld - it is the blistering hot and scalding temperatures of the netherworld.

"Okay, they are moving Zephyr's body off of the throne, and then you're going to get onto it. Got it?"

Onyx nods nervously, but a million questions remain in his eyes. "But what do I do once I get up there?"

"Just look pretty until we figure out what to do next." Onyx recoils at Evander's untimely sass, but he nods, clearly seeing that he is merely trying to lighten the mood during a doomsday scenario.

"Well go on, climb up!" Onyx nods, and starts to climb onto the platform, but the hand of a hooded figure lays a strong hand on his shoulder, jolting him away from the throne.

"Who are you? What are you doing?"

"Oh Onyx..." His name drips from her lips like poison. "Have you forgotten about me already?" The hood is removed to reveal a head of platinum-silver hair framing a pair of eyes colored by intense rage.

A kick to the back of his knee causes him to crumble to the floor, and she successfully gets to the top of the throne at the precise moment that Zephyr's body is lifted away from it. As the Disturbers hold his large, limp body in their hands, Onyx cannot help but tear his eyes away from Jade for a split second to see the remains of his previous leader. The long, bony form seems so destitute now, dangling precariously in the hands of the sorters.

"What do we do with him?" One of the more muscular sorters yells across the chasm in the direction of Evander and Onyx. A moment of clarity reveals itself to Evander, and he shrugs his shoulders in the heat of the moment, and motions toward the chasm with a dramatic point of his index finger. The sorters carrying Zephyr's limp body take one last look at their leader, and then throw his body deep into the depths of the chasm. And it falls, down, down, down, until Zephyr is no more. Even his muffled screams are absorbed into the aperture of the damned.

CHAPTER 18

Above, Jade begins to audibly cackle loudly, as the acoustics of the Great Hall amplify her voice - likely the reason that Zephyr's voice always seemed to boom over the ears of whoever was there conversing with him at that moment. The very granite pillars of the Grand Hall seem to vibrate with the presence of her excitement.

Luna catches up to Evander at the base of the throne, and tugs on his arm to get his attention. "Evander, what is happening to the Sorting Room right now? With the screens all blank?"

He turns to her and briefly yells over the noise and chaos filling the room, between the panicking Disturbers and the ever-widening chasm at their feet. "Careful of the portal, Luna. I cannot explain right now, but I have frozen the space-time continuum again until we can stabilize both realms." She nods, even though very little of that explanation makes any sense to her. A quick glance down to the widening, fiery chasm gives her all the information she needs. For now, she just stays far away from the opening in hopes to survive this revolution and resume her happy life with Onyx.

Evander looks up briefly at the throne, and he realizes that Jade is about to sit down onto it. "NO! Jade, don't do that! You will be eviscerated upon it - you do not have any ties to Earth, the current will not take to you!"

"What current?" She cackles gleefully. "There's no current here, you are just trying to scare me." And with that, Jade brazenly sits in the middle of the large throne, even kicking up her feet sacrilegiously onto the plush red armrest. “See? I’m totally fine. There’s no -”

She never gets to finish that sentence, as a look of horror registers on her face, and her skin begins to melt off of her body as her hands move to her throat in a last ditch effort for relief - which is ultimately fruitless. Her eyes bulge in agony as she screams until her vocal chords are vaporized, and the life is gone from her body. The putrid smell of her burning flesh mixes with the disgusting vapor of her fried silvery hair. What once sparkled, is now black and rotted.

The entire room goes silent for a moment, as everyone falls witness to Jade’s gory, painful death upon the very throne that their leader had inhabited until just moments ago.

Luna shrieks at the sight, and Onyx looks away as Evander squirms uncomfortably. Jade’s bones are exposed in a deathly, skeletal shadow of who she once was. After a few moments of staring at her skeleton perched on Zephyr’s throne, Evander motions for one of the other sorters to dispose of her remains into the chasm. They do so reverently, grabbing her corpse by the shoulders, and ultimately letting her bones fall deep into the Underworld, never to be reanimated again.

At this moment, Onyx realizes that by ascending that throne, he would indeed be risking his life. He tries to turn back, but then remembers his somber command to

Luna: *After all we've been through, haven't you learned? You've just got to do it afraid.*

He takes one last look at Luna in the crowd below him, and her eyes are filled with fear. He knows, without a doubt, that he could end up eviscerated just like Jade. He tries not to mourn her loss, even though she had been a friend and mentor to him for centuries. She was destroyed by her own pride and false sense of entitlement, and Onyx hopes that he is not guilty of the very same thing.

Okay. I'm going to do it afraid. Just like I told her. He takes a deep breath and then eases himself onto the plush throne, afraid of what bad thing could happen to him.

In this moment, all the fighting seems to go completely silent as he lowers himself to the throne, bracing himself for the agony of evisceration. All eyes are on him, and Luna peeks through her fingers, awaiting his fate while Evander firmly grasps her forearm protectively.

To his delight and utter relief, all the chaos seems to instantly die down as he lands on the throne – and survives. Even the portal to the Underworld shrinks considerably, and then completely closes up within a few moments. With it, the heavy wind dies down, and the temperature of the Upperworld returns to its normal tepid comfort. Some of the Upperworld beings cheer, while others look glumly down at their feet, but most are dumbfounded by the gruesome death and apocalyptic struggle they had just witnessed.

"Onyx, how are you feeling?" Evander speaks to him from the base of the throne amidst the excited chatter of the beings. Next to him stand Luna, Brielle, and Griffin, with expectant looks on their faces. The crowd in the Grand Hall begins to dissipate, and word quickly travels that the Sorting Room receptor screens are back to normal, and there are even orbs being produced again. In the lowlight of the Grand Hall, Onyx's bleach-blonde hair seems to glow, not unlike Zephyr's.

"I think I'm okay… I think, I think it worked!" Luna smiles big, and starts to climb up onto the platform of the throne to get to Onyx, but Evander stops her.

"Luna, you are not authorized to be up there. If you so much as touch that throne, you'll have a fate similar to Jade's." Luna freezes at that thought, and the realization that Jade is finally gone sinks in. She begins to break down and cry, and Onyx tries to get up to console her, but he then realizes that he is quite literally, stuck to the throne.

"Evander, do you have any idea why I cannot get off of this?" Onyx tries to hide the pained expression on his face, as not to scare Luna, but he knows that sitting here for all of eternity might be a slow and painful death for his highly intellectual needs.

Evander scratches the back of his neck while trying to think of why that might be. "If I had to guess, I would say that the life force current has joined itself to your central nervous system, which means you are physically bonded to that throne now. Have you ever noticed why Zephyr never left his throne? Now we know why."

Onyx's cerulean eyes glow with concern as he realizes the gravity of the situation. "I - I cannot sit here forever. I'm a guide, I have to help the recruits..."

"Not anymore you don't. Now, you're the Most High Being, Onyx. Your position as Head Guide has been nullified."

"But all my training! I didn't sign up for this! You brought me back against my will, and now I have to sit here. Forever? What about Luna?"

Evander steals a glance at Luna who blushes amidst the concern that is registering on her face. "What *about* Luna?" He pauses for a minute, and then he understands. "Oh... OH." He looks at her and smiles sadly, and then shrugs. "I mean, whatever thing you guys have going on, it's probably over unless Luna wants to camp out in here. And before you say anything about that, she also can't touch you. No one can, or else they'll be obliterated. It's because of the current flowing through you - it's too strong for just anyone to come into contact with."

Onyx runs his hands through his hair. "Evander, I must be honest with you - this isn't going to work for me. I'm, as you know... part humanoid, and so I have, *needs* that must be met. I cannot live like this. Luna needs me, and I need her."

"I understand but I cannot think of any way to free you. And even if I could, what would happen to the Upperworld and beyond? I think you really might just be stuck there."

Throughout all this conversation, Griffin and Brielle had been standing around, waiting for the crowds to dissipate, and they seem to be having a conversation of their own. Regardless, they both bow politely to Onyx, to which he rolls his eyes at them in response.

CHAPTER 19

"Everyone, everyone, please, settle down. I want to start by thanking you for your swift thinking and bravery during this tumultuous time as of late. Your valor has proven how truly strong the residents of the Upperworld truly are. Together, we have survived the loss of our leader, and also gained a new one - which you all have so aptly chosen. If all continues like this, we will be truly unstoppable. And you have every reason to feel so proud of that."

The crowd of the Disturbers all clap after Evander's celebratory speech during the party he hosted after the revolution took place.

"It is scary to think about what could have happened, had we not stepped it up the way we did. But we did, and it paid off. Congratulations to each and every one of you."

More clapping and whistling fills the air.

"Evander! Evander! Evander!" They begin chanting his name, during which he blushes and takes a bow awkwardly while they continue to praise his efforts.

"I cannot take the credit for this stellar achievement! Really, you must acknowledge the things you yourselves have done to get to this point, it is utterly incredible."

"And now, we can move into a brighter future, a future with a leader who does not seem to distance himself emotionally from us. A leader who genuinely cares, and has sacrificed his own needs to serve us for all eternity."

"So how is Onyx doing? Is he okay with it?" A sorter in the crowd raises his hand, with a quizzical look on his face. "I mean, it's such a big change, and if he wasn't expecting it, adjusting might be hard."

Evander swallows hard and then smiles calmly. "Well, you are right indeed that it is a big change. And there are, indeed some *stipulations* involving it, that were definitely unforeseen. But beyond that, it has been a really good thing. Once we find the right balance of everything, then it will be perfect."

Another sorter raises a hand. "But, he *does* know what he's doing, right? I mean, all our jobs are important, but generating orbs and predestining where they go, that's easily the most important. Is he definitely up to the task?"

"If he wasn't, he would have been obliterated, to put it plainly." A few gasps fly through the room. "Sorry! I didn't mean to upset you. It's just a fact though, that is all I mean. You all saw what happened to Jade."

Murmurs fill the room, but after a few moments, things settle down again in a respectful silence. Evander breaks it before everyone gets too uncomfortable. "But hey now, we're supposed to be celebrating today! There will be time to mourn the dead in a few Earth moons. Until then, please help yourself to some celebratory refreshments!"

He tries his best to inject some life back into the party, but Evander is no stranger to awkwardness. Being a record keeper of the Upperworld has undoubtedly left him with less social skills than someone like Onyx, for example, since the very essence of his job description is built on relating to and earning the trust of others. After his accidentally dark speech, everyone slowly trickles out of the room, either making the trek back to their pods for rest time, or starting their shifts in the Sorting Room or record offices.

***

While Onyx remains in the Grand Hall serving as the Most High Being, Luna finds herself working as a sorter again. The job no longer scares her, since she has been through a lot worse, and experienced a lot of different things. Some very good, like the nights with Onyx, and some very bad, like the violence and the fear she witnessed and experienced while living on Earth. Now, she is just stuck going through the motions, as she feels alone, and under stimulated. Nothing about the Sorting Room holds the allure that it once had for her. Once she felt love, and human connection far more powerful than anything she had ever felt as a sorter, she realized that she didn't miss this place as much as she had thought. Sure, the Sorting Room had become familiar, but on Earth, she was beginning to slowly adapt to a new normal - and she liked it. For the first time ever, she had agency over her own life and personality. She could love Onyx with all her heart without any backlash, and she could don clothing besides the rubbery frocks of the Upperworld. Shameful as it may seem, Luna secretly kept the Earth clothes that she and Onyx had arrived back to the Upperworld in. That purple sweater was Onyx's favorite, because he said it perfectly complimented her eyes. And it really does. Luna also kept Onyx's black and red plaid shirt and denim pants. She put those, along with her jeans, shirt, and even those silly Earth undergarments into a secret drawer in her pod. Luna desperately wanted to remember her time on Earth, and odd as it may seem to some who have never experienced Earth, those clothes will forever represent a part of her life that she would be quite loathe to forget.

She is distracted from her personal reverie by a knocking on her door. She opens it to find Brielle standing there, smiling shyly.

"Hello, Luna. I just wanted to come by and… talk, if that's okay? I can come back if it is not an opportune time…"

Luna shakes her head. "No, no, I'm fine, really. Come on in." Brielle follows her through the walkway and plops next to her on the couch in the sitting area of the pod. A few minutes of awkward silence ensues.

"So… what's going on? What can I do for you?" Luna sits back on the couch, rubbing her temples with her index fingers. She's been through a lot of stress as of late, so it makes sense that she'd be feeling at least a little tense.

"Well, um, I just wanted to talk to you about… what happened."

"Well, which thing? A lot of interesting events and occurrences have been going on lately. So you'll have to specify a little more than that."

Brielle recoils slightly from Luna's brash response, but Luna attempts to smooth it over with a kind smile. "I'm sorry, I'm just… dealing with a lot at the moment."

"Like what exactly?"

Luna exhales, and then sits up a little straighter on her side of the couch, and turns to face Brielle. "Well, living on Earth was not easy, but I came to really like it during the time I was there. It is so much different than being here, and there is so much more freedom. No schedules, or uniforms, or anything. And life is just structured so much differently."

"Wow, that sounds so… fascinating. What would you say is the biggest difference, or the thing that made the most impact on you?"

Luna looks wistfully out the window of her pod, and she can't help but think of Onyx and the love they shared. His touch, his kiss, his everything, was the most powerful sense of human emotion she had ever experienced. Unfortunately, that kind of emotion isn't really condoned in the Upperworld, for two reasons. The first and primary reason being that sorters and other Upperworld beings are not typically half-human, as Luna and Onyx are, so they do not experience complex emotions like love or attraction. Secondly, in the rare occurrence that an entity is rebooted like Onyx and Luna both were, those emotions, though very real to them, are not encouraged as they may pose as a distraction to the very important work that is accomplished in the Upperworld.

"Well, let's just say I got to… explore some things about myself that I never got to before. It was… thrilling, and powerful, and unlike anything I ever thought was possible." Luna blushes at her memories with Onyx in their house.

"Wow, that sounds amazing. What else?" Brielle perches her face on her hands, resting her elbows on her lap.

"Well, there were hard things too, of course." Luna doesn't want to remember what happened with Garth, and then consequently, Seth. She also doesn't want to think about how Seth had to be killed - unborn or not, he was her son. And in some twisted way, that is something she will always have to carry with her, for better or worse.

"Like what?" Brielle, being a younger and less-experienced sorter, clearly wants to hear anything and everything from Luna - her curious mind cannot be satiated by just the typical Upperworld knowledge.

"Well, as I said, it's painful, so I'd rather not relive it." Brielle nods apologetically and nervously rubs her hands together.

"I understand, don't worry about it."

The two sit in an uncomfortable silence for a few moments, until Luna breaks it.

"Was there something specific I could help you with? I'm sorry, I'm just… dealing with a lot at the moment, and I'm not feeling super conversational at this time."

"Oh I understand. No, I just, I guess I came by since you seemed obviously distraught earlier and I wanted to check on you. That's all, I suppose. Although, I'm not… half humanoid like you, so I probably won't ever experience emotions like that. But looking at you now, I'm thinking that might be for the best."

Luna nods politely, even though most of what this younger girl says is often a bit harsher than she likely intends. She's got a good heart, but her inherent inability to feel complex emotions definitely shows itself to Luna.

EPILOGUE

"Hey, Onyx." He looks up to see the small form of his one-true-love, Luna, looking up at him from the floor directly in front of the throne in the Grand Hall.

"Oh, hello Luna." He smiles even though he's been bored out of his mind, and uncomfortably stationed on the highest chair in existence.

"How have you been?" She asks politely, even though she already knows the answer.

"Oh, just fabulous. Basically, I just sit here while the world goes on without me. But on the bright side, I don't actually feel the need to sleep anymore! Evander suggested it could be something about the life-force current flowing through me, I'm not totally sure. It is unfortunate though, since sleeping would be a great pastime."

Luna forces herself to smile at his attempt at positivity, but it is getting more and more difficult. She's been visiting him in the Grand Hall just about every day, and it has been so difficult because they cannot get too close, or even take a leisurely walk in the comfortingly familiar purple fog of the Upperworld.

"Onyx? I miss you."

He smiles sadly. "I miss you too, Luna."

"Do you think… I'll ever get to love you again?"

Onyx smiles again, this time with less pain and more sympathy, thinking about how his new employment has left her feeling at a loss as well.

"Well, honestly, I don't know how you can without being obliterated." Onyx smiles at his own joke, but Luna remains pensive, and clearly not enthused.

"Yes, I know. But... you can't really sit there *forever* right? That'd be crazy..."

Onyx sighs. "Unfortunately, it's not all that crazy. I'm taking over for Zephyr, remember? And he didn't exactly have a social life beyond this chair, so why would I get to?"

"But you're the Head Guide! That is your *job*..."

"*Was* my job. Now apparently, my job is sitting here, doing nothing for all eternity." Onyx looks down at his feet, since he hates letting Luna see him cry.

Luna moves a couple paces closer to him, but then stops herself before she accidentally touches him or the throne. This new arrangement is destroying them, and neither of them can escape.

"Well, I still love you, Onyx. I always will. And I'm happy, at least we had the time together on Earth that we did. We'll always have... the memories..." Now Luna begins to openly sob, and Onyx is enraged that he cannot get down off of his throne and comfort her the way he has, even since day one of her existence.

"Luna, this is utterly ridiculous. I will get off of here, someday, somehow."

"But you'll put the entire Upperworld in jeopardy! Besides, you couldn't get off of there even if you wanted to - you are literally stuck."

"I know, but I *have to. I absolutely have to.* I cannot live like this.

Luna nods, but she frowns, because she cannot think of any possible solution to fix their problem. It is an unfixable dilemma, and even if he could get off that chair, Onyx would do the right thing and stay, because he always puts the good of humanity before himself. He always has, and he always will.

"Onyx. Onyx!" Luna turns around to see Griffin running down the Grand Hall toward the throne room. His excited voice bounces off of the bare stone surfaces of the columns and ornate decor.

"Hello, Griffin. What can I do for you?" Onyx tries to smile, but this business of faking it is destroying him inside. Very soon, he worries he'll become as stoic and cold as Zephyr was.

"Onyx! You are never going to believe this, but I think I can help you!"

His bright blue eyes widen, but he is loathe to get his own hopes up. "Help me… what?"

"I think I can let you get off the chair without putting the realms in danger!"

Onyx frowns and shakes his head. "That's impossible, Griffin. Although I appreciate your attempt, that's very thoughtful of you."

"No, I mean I actually have a way. I've already worked it all out and everything."

Luna looks over to Griffin. "Seriously? Please don't tease me, I just can't handle it if you are."

"Yeah, I've got it. Allow me to explain. Actually, Evander, get in here!"

Evander saunters into the Grand Hall upon Griffin's signal, and he carries with him a digital sketch board with some thoughts mapped out on it. "Hello, Onyx. Hope you've enjoyed the throne, but we're about to get you off of it."

"I sincerely hope you can." The mock enthusiasm drips from Onyx's lips.

"Oh, we will. It's as simple as this." Evander sets the digital board in front of Onyx and Luna. "It was your idea, Griffin, after all. Why don't you do the honors?"

Griffin cannot hide the smile creeping onto his face. "Okay! So basically, the reason Onyx is stuck on the throne and untouchable is because the life force current is flowing through him - the power source for him as the Most High Being. However, we are looking to create sort of a wireless set up, so that the current stays in the chair, and Onyx can continue to produce the orbs remotely."

"Does that mean I can hug him again?"

Evander rolls his eyes, but smiles. "Yes, Luna. You can go back to business as usual as soon as it's all set.

"Wait a second here. This all seems far too good to be true. How in the Upperworld do you intend to pull this off?"

Griffin smiles. "By going back into your past. The answers we need are *in your past*."

"There isn't much to tell, I've just been a Head Guide here, you know that."

"No, not that past. I mean the past before that past."

Onyx and Luna exchange confused glances. Evander steps slightly closer to explain.

"We're talking about what happened *before* any of that. That's right, we are going back to Earth year 1790 to visit your *mother*."

Onyx's face blushes bright red, and he looks down at his feet in embarrassment. "I didn't know you knew the extent of that, Griffin."

Evander chimes in to explain. "I told him, I am a record keeper, after all. I figured you wouldn't mind, since it might just be the thing to set you free without causing the entire Upperworld to descend into the Underworld." Evander scratches the back of his neck, hoping he has not offended Onyx, but their friendship extends far beyond the formality that Onyx has had to recently adopt.

"Okay, so what good is that going to accomplish?"

"That's simple. Your tie to the life-force current is linked to your pre-Upperworld past, because part of your qualifications for the position involve a link to Earth, which in your case, is your humanoid-conception. If we can trace back the exact moment your history changed -"

Griffin cuts in. "- in this case, that could be the moment your mother decided to abort you, then we can take that snapshot of history and input that into the system. This is what we would call a 'major turning point' - it is like a key to sort of 'break the rules', so to speak. There is a lot of power in that one moment."

"Okay, so say you find the exact moment. Then what do you do?"

Evander smiles. "Then we pause time momentarily, just long enough to input the time coordinates into the main system of the Upperworld's processing system. And just like that, you'll be free. The orbs will keep flowing, but you can lead a more normal life, maybe even be a guide again, if you want to."

Onyx and Luna exchange a knowing look, and neither of them can hide the smiles on their faces.

"This sounds…" Luna pauses to find the right word, and Onyx finishes for her.

"… amazing. Let's try it."

Explore a forbidden past to find the moment that will set him free...

The Rise of Onyx

The conclusion to

The Upperworld Series

Coming Fall 2018

Exclusive First Look:

Luna's calm footfalls fill the acoustics of the Grand Hall, where Onyx has been charged with the responsibility of producing enough orbs to keep the entire human population from dying out. She approaches him, smiling, despite his extreme boredom and feelings of utter despondency.

"Hello, Onyx."

He lifts his head up from where it was resting on the back of the throne, and looks down at her with weary, eyes not unlike a cloudy blue sky.

"Hello, Luna."

She walks a bit closer to him, just reveling in his presence even though she must stay far away from the current that runs through him now. A silence loaded with desperation fills the space between them, as the human portions of their hybrid forms become desperate for each other.

"How is… everything here going?" She motions to the area around the throne, but Onyx understands that she means everything in the Sorting room, as well as the orb production.

"Just fine, I think. I'm new at this, but I am also getting quite tired of it."

Luna tilts her head slightly. "You're tired? I thought you don't get tired anymore, because of the current? At least, that's what you told me before."

Onyx shakes his head. "Well, I don't get *physically* tired anymore, perhaps that is what I meant. Sitting here, and not really doing anything, is quickly wearing on me."

Luna nods, and frowns sadly. "Well, it's important, what you're doing, you know. You saved *all of us*."

Onyx sighs. "I know, but I do wish I had the chance to make that choice on my own. I was volunteered to do this, and even though I didn't know what I was getting into and didn't really want to, there was not time to find a suitable replacement before the entire Upperworld would be sucked into the portal."

"Well, *I* think you are amazing. I really do."

"That makes one of us."

Luna takes a step closer to the throne.

"Not too close Luna, I'm dangerous. Don't forget that. I could not live with myself if I…." He cannot even bring himself to finish that sentence, but he counters with another one instead. "No wonder Zephyr always seemed so cold. This is a miserable existence."

"Maybe it's worse for you because you are part humanoid."

Onyx nods. "It is possible. Although, I guess we'll never truly know about Zephyr's origin. Not that it matters now – he is long gone."

She hastily changes the subject before Onyx gets too upset again. "Well, Evander and Griffin are working to get you out of there, isn't that exciting! There is so much to be grateful for, Onyx. I'm grateful for this. I'm grateful for the chance to have you back, even though nothing is guaranteed."

Onyx brushes a piece of his short blonde hair out of his eyes. "You and me both, Luna. Any day now, I am trying to remind myself I'll be freed. But it is steadily getting harder and harder to fully believe that."

"I understand, I really do. But you have to stay positive, please? Can you do that, at least for me?" Luna is not accustomed to being the stronger one – as long as she has existed, it has always been Onyx to make her stronger and keep her safe. Now it is her turn to do the same for him, and she's not used to the responsibility it holds.

"I'm going to try, Luna. That's the best I can say about that right now. Beyond that, I really don't know." He runs his hand through his bleach-blonde hair and sighs again.

"Whatever happens, we'll at least be able to say we tried."

"That is true, but oh my pod I really do hope it works. I can't do this forever. I just can't."

Special thanks to my very talented friend Joel for helping me polish up that epic fight scene between Onyx and Seth! Couldn't have done it without you ☺

ANGELINA SINGER is a college student studying English, Music, and of course, Creative Writing. In her spare time she enjoys crocheting, and mentoring younger music students at a local music store where she has been studying guitar for nearly a decade. She views her writing as a way to simultaneously escape from and embrace reality, especially through the twisted labyrinth of a dystopian setting as seen in *The Upperworld Series*.

Facebook: @AngelinaSingerAuthor
Blog: angelinasingerauthor.wordpress.com
Amazon: https://www.amazon.com/Angelina-Singer/e/B0743ZF23N/ref=dp_byline_cont_book_1

Book one of the Upperworld Series: The Sorting Room

Who decides where we are born and who we love? Luna is an immortal entity in the Upperworld learning how to assign human souls to the body and life they're intended for. Onyx is her mentor and guide there, teaching her everything she needs to know about assigning souls and dispatching them to Earth. Everything goes well until Luna's friend makes a major mistake and Luna is sent to Earth after covering for her. In her absence, an unbelievable secret is revealed that changes everything she thought she knew about how the world works. Will Luna survive long enough on Earth to fix things? Or will she succumb to the pressures and pitfalls of living life as a human girl before the entire system unravels?

https://www.amazon.com/dp/1546936637/ref=nav_timeline_asin?_encoding=UTF8&psc=1

Available now on Amazon in paperback and digitally for Kindle!
Reviews are greatly appreciated.

Also by Angelina Singer...

JUST LIKE A PILL

When Scarlett gets a sinus infection the week before Homecoming, she never knew that she would be plunged deep into a tangled mess involving the hunky guitar player, Maxx, who goes to her school. She quickly develops a mysterious side effect that appears to cause Maxx to be instantly attracted to her. With her health-freak fashionista friend Izzy by her side, Scarlett searches desperately to find answers about the sketchy "antibiotics" that she took to combat her symptoms. The time clock is set to one week, and between dodging the fiendish escapades of the high school "it-girl" who dates Maxx, as well as the feeble advances of nerdy Greg, Scarlett has to figure out what's real and what's not before anyone she cares about gets hurt.

ALSO AVAILABLE on Amazon and Kindle!

Any reviews would be great!

https://www.amazon.com/dp/1533537941/ref=nav_timeline_asin?_encoding=UTF8&psc=1

10822963R00141

Made in the USA
Lexington, KY
02 October 2018